GW00862991

Wine Dark, Sea Blue

Dear Ted,

Hear you're doing well!

Hope to see you

soon,

A.L. Michael

Stairwell Books

Published by Stairwell Books
70 Barbara Drive
Norwalk
CT 06851 USA

Wine Dark, Sea Blue©2013 A.L. Michael and Stairwell Books

All rights reserved. No part of this publication may be reproduced,
stored in or introduced into a retrieval system, or transmitted, in
any form, or by any means (electronic, mechanical, photocopying,
recording, e-book or otherwise) without the prior written permission
of the author. Any person who does any unauthorised act in
relation to this publication may be liable to criminal prosecution
and civil claims for damages. Purchase of this book in e-book
format entitles you to store the original and one backup for your
own personal use: it may not be re-sold, lent or given ·away to
other people and it may only be purchased from the publisher or
an authorised agent.

This book is sold subject to the condition that it shall not, by way of
trade or otherwise, be lent, resold, hired out, or otherwise
circulated without the author's prior consent in any form of binding
or cover other than that in which it is published and without a
similar condition including this condition being imposed on the
subsequent purchaser.

ISBN: 978-1-939269-03-4

Printed and bound in the United Kingdom by Russell Prrss

Layout design: Alan Gillott
Cover art: Joseph Mauk

Acknowledgements

In memory of Dorothy Levy, the first person to tell me I could do this.

And for my grandmothers. Just because.

Chapter One

My mother's voice was on repeat as my brain lining trembled and began to disintegrate.

'Accidental overdose, the paramedics said.'

'How the fuck is that possible?'

'She was getting older, so many different medications...' Mum's voice was tinny, lost down the phone line in the white noise. She forgot to tell me off for swearing, and her voice trailed into sighs and silence.

'What do you need me to do?'

'Get home now,' she said and hung up. It was ten am, and Mum never called before twelve. I should have known when the phone rang. There's never good news before twelve. Especially not after half a gram of MDMA and almost an entire bottle of vodka, shared in a South London flat with a boy whose name I'd already forgotten. He was pretending to be asleep when I took the call, and I was grateful. I paced the small space of his flat, bare feet scratching on his carpet, waiting to see how I felt, if I would feel anything at all. If I would panic when I didn't.

He made a big show of waking up, yawning and stretching. He looked much like all the others, dark hair, nice arms. His smile failed to hide a concerned expression.

'Everything okay?' As he stood, his jeans slid down to his hips. A thin line of hair ran down from his belly button to the start of his boxers, and I focused on that. A dark trail of ants, a line not to cross, a line of coke, a line in the sand. Give me a line, a lifeline, anything.

'What's your name again?'

He smirked and ran a hand through his hair, 'Daniel.'

'Right, Daniel.'

I tried to place that somewhere amongst the memories of the night before, of the breathless laughter and the way I stroked his fingertips. The guitar sat untouched in the corner of the room. He hadn't played for me. His fingertips were flat and rough, and I had traced his filed-down nails in soft delight. He was amazing last night. They always are.

But in the little white-flaked flat, with the green curtains that tinted the daylight, I felt like I was looking at this Daniel person from far away, through a haze of heat distortion. Like I understood that humans were just walking, talking lumps of meat, much like every other animal that lived and died. Except humans had things like Topshop and SkyPlus and Hello Magazine. This Daniel person was just another part of that world.

'My grandmother's dead,' I said, staring past him to the posters on the wall. They were in French, *pretentious twat*. I scanned his bookshelf for Sartre and Nietzsche, and found them, broken spines and folded pages. Last night he was my best friend, this Daniel.

'Are you okay?' He started towards me, and I stepped back, 'sorry, stupid question.' He detoured to the sink, ran the tap, and handed me a glass of water. I drank desperately, so that I felt it hit my insides, rebounding off my organs and making waves. My stomach was an ocean. But it was always that way on the comedown. Nothing was different, not the boy, or the drugs, or the Saturday morning feeling. Except that she was dead.

Moving took forever, each muscle moaning, telling me I was stupid to do anything but lie down and get warm. Slow motion. Cotton wool head. Fuzzy.

Daniel was kind and earnest, like a lot of them are, willing to chat, eager to carry on the party. Some are like

2

me, and happily say goodbye in the morning, not expecting anything more that a one-night friendship. Some are ashamed. Most of the time they're asleep, and I just pick up my bag from by the door and get out. There are rules.

'I've got to go.'

'Maybe have a cup of tea first, eh?' His voice had a northern drawl, soft around the vowels. I hadn't noticed it last night, hidden behind the clipped London sound.

'I don't...' I shook my head, surprised by how lost I felt, 'I'm numb. Completely numb.'

'That's the comedown. You *do* know that? Last night, you said you knew. Chemical imbalance, body fuck-up. Right?' He reached out a hand, and I backed away.

'I know, I do know. I just...'

'Shock.' He nodded intently, and moved closer, almost whispering. 'Look, I'm going to make us a nice cup of tea, and we'll sit for a bit, and you can go when you're ready, okay?'

He'd reached me by that point, and I couldn't stop my teeth from chattering, my hands from shaking. So cold, ridiculously cold. How was he shirtless, the bloody idiot.

He wrapped his arms around me, his cold palms flat against the base of my spine. You don't do that on the comedown. The night before is for touching. Loving the sensation of hands on shoulders, fingertips encircling wrists. Skin on skin isn't right the morning after. You're back in your cocoon, and every other human is a hundred lightyears from where you are. He could have been anyone, but he was warm, and that was enough. And I put my arms around him, encouraging him to hold me tighter, harder, because if I was going to fall apart, it may as well be when someone was holding me up. It was only when I had to gasp for air that I finally pushed him away.

'Don't confuse what this is.'

'And what *is* this, exactly?' His smile was a half-twitch at the corner of his mouth, like I was a child he was humouring because he wanted to see what funny thing I did next

'This is two people who got fucked together, and in the morning said goodbye.' I strode past him, and grabbed my bag from the floor. Purple party bag, always ready for the escape. Toothbrush, fresh from a pack of ten, four of which are remaining. Ancient Nirvana hoody with the smiley face symbol peeling off. Scarf, always useful. Large bottle of water, because it helps. Chewing gum for the gurn, painkillers more for the placebo than the effect. The comedown kit.

'Ellie.' Daniel smiled and shook his head.

'Don't say my name like that!'

'Like what?'

'Like you know one fucking thing about me!' I pulled on my hoody, tugging on the hood and pulling my hair free. My hand rested on the door handle.

'I was listening last night when you spoke.' His smile was smug, his hands open, palms up.

'I hate to burst your bubble, but this is a weekly occurrence for me. You're just one of many guys I do this with. It doesn't mean anything. Ships in the night, strangers on a pill. Get it?'

The door handle was warm and slippery.

'You really think you won't remember this moment?'

I rolled my eyes in response, 'Sorry, guess you're just not that special.'

4

'Your grandmother's dead. You always remember where you are when there's bad news.'

'Well, maybe I don't care. Or I don't like my family. Maybe I have no family.'

Daniel took two lazy steps and was invading my space. I tried not to breathe in, because it was his air. Hold your breath, Elena. Get out, go home, deal with everything. Everything. Her. Deal with whatever that means.

'You,' he smiled, 'are a terrible liar.' He stepped back a little, and I got the full effect of that smile. A smile that dared me to argue, that wanted me angry instead of scared. Anything but numb.

'I like you,' he said, stepping back, that half-twitch grin in place again, 'So, tea.'

He strode across the room, and tapped an ancient green kettle with his foot, so it lit up and hissed. His little kitchen area was so tidy, an ageing mug on the side with a knife and a spoon sitting in it, his one plate in the sink pathetic and lonely. I knew then that I'd stay.

I had the chance to walk out, slam the door, but what would I be heading towards, really? Parents who didn't know what I'd been doing when my grandmother died. What was so important that I hadn't come home, they would ask. Family who thought my nights out included a couple of glasses of wine, maybe a kiss. The night spent on Dexter's floor, or in Lee's spare room. Never class As and a one-night friendship, in bed with a boy in Clapham Junction. Never that I did it every week, every chance I could, because it made me feel so perfectly alive until the morning came.

So I dropped the bag. I sat on the bed and drank strong tea from a chipped blue mug. I watched rubbish re-runs on TV and smiled, even laughed. I forgot. And when he relit a joint from the night before, I let him rest his head next to mine, closing my eyes as he softly blew the smoke into my mouth. Sweet, herby, tinted by toothpaste. Sleepy green, taking the edge off of the morning.

When I finally did leave, that morning sun had faded into grey dullness. I felt flushed with and irritable as I walked to the tube, pushing the last moments with Daniel from my mind. He'd asked for my phone number, and I'd given it to him. I never gave them my phone number, I only wanted them when they were strangers. I only ever wanted one night with someone who had no idea who I was. But when he kissed my cheek, he smelled of sweat and aftershave, and everything I'd found fascinating the night before. I had let him hold me in his bed as I pretended to cry, pretended to feel anything. But all I felt was cold. And he was so warm. The warm boy with the cold hands.

I walked through Clapham Common to the tube station, and got on the Northern Line. It had been hours since Mum called. When I finally appeared Dad would rant about my irresponsible nature, my selfishness. Mum would be disappointed, and that's always worse.

The train carriage was empty, and I sat in a corner seat with my headphones in. I was glad there were no people, I can't bear to make eye contact on the tube. On those kinds of Saturday mornings, I start to get paranoid about the Underground. I take it personally when people choose the seat two down from me, or move when another space becomes available. Like they think I'll infect them. I never move seats in case I hurt someone's feelings.

I tugged on my hood again, and put my headphones in. Sometimes, I pretend to react to the music I'm not hearing, smile when I play a certain song on my internal jukebox, tap my feet in time to a rhythm that isn't there.

This time, I just closed my eyes, and tried not to think about how many people's arses had sat on the seat I was sitting on.

The train droned on, rattled and jolted and it was easy to lose myself. I watched at every stop how the tourists boarded the opposite trains, heading into town for a weekend with the family, a day out with friends. That was the best thing about returning from central on a Saturday, everyone was going in the other direction.

I wobbled out of the tube station at High Barnet and walked to the bus stop. The sky promised rain. I told myself I would let five buses go passed, then I'd get on the sixth and go home. Give me five buses, thirty minutes. Breathing space.

Dead. She was dead, and I had been smiling with a stranger. Had she died whilst I was dancing? I shivered, it felt like I was drowning in mundanity, greyness. Traffic, and jobs and so many people just living their little lives. Overdose. She never seemed that old to me. I thought of her dark eyes, her white hair, her steady trundle across a room with her swollen ankles. Overdoses were ugly. Painful.

I suddenly wanted to be back in Daniel's little white room with the green curtains, where time froze and I had no dead relatives. I didn't have to be strong in that room. But I did now. I waited till the seventh bus came and went. Then I walked home.

Chapter Two

'Kounia, bella, omorfi go-bell-a!'

The words make no sense, but they've been here forever. Yiayia sits me in her lap, that strange stronghold with her chubby arms around me. As she sings the lullaby she rocks me back and forth, and I know that when it gets to the end she's going to lean me back off her lap, so far that I'll scramble for her, so sure I'll fall.

This is her song, always in this big green chair, overstuffed and uncomfortable, with the crocheted blanket over the arm. I will hear her sing this song to multiple babies in the future, swing them back and forth as she swings me now. I'll laugh when I'm older, forget how scary it is for that one moment when you think no-one will catch you. She always does, but I never stop being scared.

'Koun-ia! Bella! Omorfi go-bell-a!'

Her singing speeds up, becomes more staccato and her smile is so bright, so close. Her voice is sweet, if deep and a little rough. Her hair is still dark, and I can't even tell how long ago that must have been, if I'm really recalling her, or just the photographs. I can't remember how old I am because she's always done this, and she always will, until I'm too old to sit on her lap anymore.

We call it the Big Old House, because that's what it is. Huge, and daunting, and always dark. It always smells of olive oil and whatever Yiayia's cooking that day. Big pots of soup bubbling on the stove. Always the faint scent of frying and old carpet. Even as she rocks me, I'm holding an apple, huge and shiny, she's shined with her red apron that sits across the back of the armchair. She rocks me back again and I drop the apple on the floor. It thuds dully and rolls.

She smiles at me, a mischievous grin that I don't think I'll ever see again.

'You do on purpose, make me stop, eh kori?' She reaches down to pick up the apple, and I start to slip. Her reflexes are fast, and she pulls me to her quickly, gathers me up and holds me close until I'm unable to see around her. I'm hot and it's dark and I can't breathe, but it's safe. I'm still.

'I never drop you dahlink, is okay,' she shushes me, arms heavily around me, 'you never fall. Promise.'

She plants a sticky kiss on my forehead, and starts the song again.

Chapter Three

'Is your Dad ready?' Mum asked Nicky as he loped down the stairs. Nicky loped everywhere, too tall, too broad, always trying to hide in the background, which was impossible.

'I think he's on the phone.'

The three of us stood in silence, dressed in black. I stepped into my patent shoes, and they pinched already, squeaking on the floorboards. Too late to change now, besides, something about painful shoes at a funeral felt appropriate, like penance, or an acute sense of perspective. Yeah, your feet hurt, but you could be dead.

Nicky nudged me with a sad little smile on his face, offering his tie. His shirt was half-untucked, and his jacket was creased. When he took his hands from his pockets, there was fluff stuck to his fingertips. I wondered if the last time he wore that suit was to our grandfather's funeral. That had been years ago, no wonder it looked so worn. It was unlike Mum to let that stuff pass, to let him wear an old suit, to let him look bedraggled. But she was busy looking up the stairs with hope, as if at any moment Dad would emerge and tell us that everything would be alright. And Nicky never really looked right in a suit anyway. You could only do so much.

'Come here,' I tiptoed as my brother bent down, and started working on the tie, loops and over, straighten then tighten. I never made it quite tight enough. Putting Nicky in a tie was like suffocating him, he'd spend all day batting at it, like a dog with a new collar. 'Sorted.'

'Cheers,' he thumbed my elbow, 'are you doing a reading?'

'No, are you?'

'They didn't ask me, they asked you.' He smiled a little, nudging me. *Step up, go on, say something nice, say anything.*

'I just...can't.'

Part of me considered that I just had nothing to say. She was here and then she was gone. My grandmother, my *Yiayia*. Blinked out of existence at sixty-six. And I didn't feel a fucking thing.

'It's okay, El, don't worry about it.' He kissed my cheek and moved over to Mum, who was scanning a list she'd made, double-checking everything, trying to avoid panicking about whether there'd be enough food at the wake, or who'd take Auntie Maria to the church. Nicky put an arm around her, and I visibly saw her relax.

He was kind, my brother, he assumed it was stage fright, that I didn't want to get up in front of all those people and break down. But it was worse than that. Because I would get up there, and talk about her, and I wouldn't shed a tear. I couldn't miss her. I couldn't even comprehend she was gone. She could be in the Big Old House, pottering around in the dark, making pastries, cooking soup. Or she was tying back the purple velvet curtains to let the slightest bit of light into the dullness. And what about the house? Did anyone think about that? Nicky should get it, really, eldest grandchild. Her was her carer. Had been her carer. And what would he do now? No job, no-one to care for, to stay with? Would he have to move home again? She must have promised him something. But promises are just words, and they die as easily as people.

'Elena! *Ade, chkk, chkk!*' My mother clapped her hands, telling me to hurry up. Sometimes it was easy to forget Mum wasn't Greek. She'd become one of them over the years, gradually ingratiating herself, speaking the language better than my Father. She was the one who made Greek food, who lead the dances, sang along with

11

the *bouzoukia*. She had visited my grandmother, spent hours chatting away in that language I could never understand.

She didn't look like them, Mum. Fair skin and bright red hair that made her stand out in the sea of olive skin, dark hair, and dark eyes. She was different. She used to wear colourful clothes, and beads that jangled along her freckled wrists, announcing her entrance into a room. Hearing the way she spoke their language was always a little alarming.

She used to tell me about her childhood, growing up in Tullamore, how she wanted more than anything to get away from a tiny town where everyone knew what you were thinking and planning and doing. She ran away. 'Got out of there before I was knee-high to a grasshopper,' she used to say. No-one could pin her down, keep her trapped, keep her small. She wanted the world.

But as I looked at her, in the smart black dress she'd agonised over (was it too short, too dressy, too uncomfortable?), with her fading auburn hair pulled back violently, I noticed the change with a jolt. She was a pale, little woman worrying about whether there was enough food to stop people saying we were stingy, if *Theo* Andreas and *Theo* Gigi would be able to hold out through the service before arguing. If Auntie Helena would make a comment because Mum's shoes weren't completely black. She put on another layer of powder from her compact, and it made her even paler. Her beaded bracelets sat on top of the microwave, because no-one wanted attention at a funeral. No-one wanted noise, or colour or happiness.

She fretted away to herself, worrying about things that were irrelevant, about what the family would say about us. She had become one of them. I wondered if she even knew.

At the funeral, no-one called me Ellie. Only Elena. The same chattering voices, over and over with the same empty condolences. Round, made-up faces with long dark hair harshly highlighted or starkly greying. It would have been so easy to let them fade into one wailing person, one person who insisted on saying the most stupid, irrelevant bullshit to avoid an awkward conversation.

They loved to tell me things I already knew.

'You name after her! She be so proud they call you Elena!'

'Strong, good woman, you have her name! Is lucky, have her name.'

'Elena is strong name, good name. Why you call yourself Ellie? Ellie is *ingleso* name, has no history, no culture! Why you choose name like that?'

This came from the older generations of Aunties I hadn't seen in years, and every answer was 'yes, *Thea*, no *Thea*, of course.' For these people, if your name wasn't someone else's, it wasn't worth anything. The more modern mothers might have chosen English names, but for the most part, you were named after your parent or you grandparent. I was the first girl, they had no choice, I was destined to be named after *Yiayia*. Mum didn't fight it, Irish family wasn't so different. You are named for your ancestor, to carry on their legacy. Their life lives on through yours. I wasn't 'Little Elena' anymore, I was now simply 'Elena', the only one remaining.

The funeral was dark and lonely, chanted in words I only understood in my sleep. Their prayers were warbled half-songs, and I watched Nicky for the cues to make the sign of the cross, to repeat 'amen'. The priest stared out from

13

behind dark eyes and grey beard, his black robes swaying with the righteousness of this God I never knew.

The church was stone cold, and despite every wooden pew being filled with black-clad relatives, it felt far too big to ever be filled. Hundreds of people could have loved her, could turn up to pay their respects and yet it would never be enough to make it seem full. The incense was thick, and though it smelled like weddings and christenings, it stung my eyes and choked me. The gold cross around my neck was warm and heavy, and it occurred to me I'd only ever worn it for funerals.

The only way I could start to cry was to picture her body in that tiny little wooden box, so small, too small. Consciously feel the pads of her fingertips, worn from needlework. Visualise each line on her face, each varicose vein protruding from behind her swollen knees. *She's in there, she's in there.*

And by the time the retching started, the swollen nose and stinging eyes, it was time to line up and kiss and kiss and kiss all these strangers' cheeks, family or not, and hear them say how sorry sorry sorry they were until I resented existing and was sorry for that, too. And even though you never properly got to cry, you have to stop, pull yourself up without wobbling on your heels, because you're very aware of this parade of over-done, dark-skinned people, and of them saying 'I'm sorry', and you saying 'thank you'. I thank these people a hundred times for saying the only thing they can say.

Then we move from the church to the poky hall next door, and the priest blesses the food in the name of this magical ghost, and his daddy and his son, then happily sits there chomping away at half of it as payment. No-one can say the church doesn't have a fair system of loss and gain.

After that the drink starts to flow, and it becomes more like a party, except there are no funny stories, no embarrassing moments. People can only talk about her kindness.

Another 'once removed' Auntie remarks that *Yiayia* is with my grandfather now, and Gali whispers, 'God help her.'

I almost laugh, and pinch her under the table. She sits next to me and grasps my hand too tightly, like when we were kids. I remember holding her hand at our grandfather's funeral, when Nicky wasn't there to look after us. She was my cousin by blood, but I called her my sister. Her memories were my memories, and we mourned together, each with a glass of wine as everyone else seemed to talk way too fast, way too much. We blankly listened as the Aunties happily chatted away about their botox, their laser-eye surgery, the stupid shit their dumb-fuck kids had achieved, and I wanted to scream. *This should be about her.*

There was nothing of Yiayia there, sitting in fold-up chairs at the tables they use for Greek school on Saturdays. Eating hardened sandwiches and oddly cut bits of celery, while people talked for the sake of filling the silence.

'So Elena, finished Uni? What are you doing now?'

Mourning my grandmother, what are you doing now?

'Working in an art gallery in Pimlico,' I replied. I always said it exactly like that, so it sounded important. So no-one quizzed me on the day-to-day tasks of mopping the floor and stopping teenagers on school trips from shagging in the disabled toilet.

'Well, isn't that exciting, our little artiste!' Unknown Aunty replied, and moved on to Gali, waiting for something she could jump in with a story about her own children.

'What about you, darling?'

'I'm an assistant at a production company,' Gali smiled quietly, and her eyes met mine. She was cleaning toilets too. Along with fetching tea, and getting her arse grabbed by the copywriters.

Unknown Aunty didn't even think to ask if we were getting paid for those jobs, and we let her assume we were actually getting somewhere in the world, not working for nothing in the hopes of a lucky break, where one day someone would turn around and see how brilliant we were.

I made to leave, but Gali clutched at my hand. I widened my eyes, and motioned Nicky over.

Unknown Aunty had started talking about someone she knew who was a weather girl, and might be going on Big Brother. Nicky provided a distraction as I headed out for some fresh air. If I'd dragged Gali with me we could have shared a cigarette, like we had when we were teenagers, hidden behind cough sweets and perfume. Even into our twenties, smoking in front of family never felt okay.

My father stopped me en-route, teary-eyed. 'Darling, darling, it's a sad day.'

I refrained from rolling my eyes, because what else was he going to say.

'You've been very quiet today, letting it be about your grandmother. I'm proud of you for that.'

I accepted the damp kiss on both cheeks, and that dull ache in my stomach like he thought I'd do something to make this day worse.

'She's a good girl, Elena, strong, like my mother,' I heard him tell someone as I walked away, pride in his voice, 'she can be a bit argumentative though, been raised like an English girl, stubborn.'

My mother looked up from across the room, where I stood still, unsure of where to go, what to do, who they needed me to be. She raised an eyebrow. *Are you okay?*

I nodded to my father and rolled my eyes, and she shrugged in response, a little smile.

Let him have his time on stage, let him tell the stories.

The stories would change over time, the things he remembered would become brighter, more interesting. The details, the truth would be lost in his loving nostalgia. Sizes and numbers would be exaggerated, faults would be erased. He would tell the same stories over and over, and each time his mother's legacy would become more unreachable. She would cease to be a woman, and become a legend. We'd forget about the small things in the face of these big fairy stories.

I stumbled in the stupid shoes, fetching tea for people, smiling blandly as they patted my shoulder, called me a good girl. Be quiet, be stupid, be invisible. And I knew if it was anyone else's final shindig, it would *Yiayia* who would be fetching the tea, checking everyone had enough to eat. So at least I had a role to fill.

When the last few people were leaving, and I'd collected up all the grey cups and saucers for washing up, I was exhausted with the sounds of people's voices, of their stories, their embellishments, their empty achievements. A sob hung in my chest like a pendulum. I grabbed my bag and felt around the worn inside for rip in the fabric. Inside that was a baggie. And inside the baggie was a screwed up piece of rizzler. I closed the kitchen door, scooped out the minute remainder of white powder, and rubbed it into my gums. Leaning over kitchen counter, eyes on the door, it was a rush. It tasted speedy, a little like baking soda, and I rubbed my gums roughly, catching the flesh on my nails. I swore as I bled into my mouth, dribbling into a half-full teacup. I watched as the red drops separated briefly into the beige liquid, then sank. I briefly wondered if her blood was my blood. If it was her blood in a greying chipped teacup in a church hall. It was a depressing thought.

I licked my lips and set to washing up as the grit of the powder went down the back of my throat like bile. I tried to imagine what she'd think of me if she was here. But she wasn't, so what did it matter, really?

Chapter Four

'Elena,' she smiles, drawing out the 'l' of my name, our name. I only answer to it when she says it. When Dad calls me that, I'm being told off. When anyone else does, it doesn't feel like me, a completely different person. A good little Greek girl.

We're sitting in the back garden of the Big Old House, perching on the stone steps, and it's sunny but cold. The garden is as it always is, green and lush, overgrowing. I like to pretend it's the secret garden, that I can creep about in the bracken and the long grass, and no-one can ever see me. It's my hiding place, and one of the best things about going to Yiayia's.

She hands me a few grapes from the spindly vine that grows by the back window, they're soft and a little sharp, but somehow, not so bad. She cuts the wide, flat leaves from the vine with a sharp knife, little flash of metal. The same knife she uses to peel the potatoes, or cut my apple into pieces.

'Important, *kori*, look,' she cuts in sharp strokes, leaving no torn leaves or split branches, 'as soon as grapes down, cut. If no, it pull down whole vine, then...'

She frowns, searching for the word, but I'm used to the pauses, I like to guess, to help her find the word.

'What you call it, dahlink?'

'What, Yiayia?'

'Boom,' her hands expand outwards like an explosion, then she nods, 'ah. Chaos, it make chaos.'

I dig my fingers into the soft, cool soil. It rained last night, and the whole garden smells like spring. I touch the vine leaves, slightly furry and completely different from how they are when we eat them as *koubebia, Yiayia's* speciality. It amazes me that something I've eaten forever is actually made from leaves.

'What's that stick for?' I poke it, the small stick that the vine gently wraps itself around.

'For root, make root grow up.' She points to show me 'up', our little sign language. She has to try extra hard with me, with Nicky or Gali she could speak in Greek, but I'm the youngest, and I never learnt. Nicky used to come home with horror stories of the priests who ran Greek school, and I swore I'd never go. They scared me, with their wiry beards and dark eyes, and big black robes. I hid under the dining room table when my parents tried to make me go, and I'll regret that forever. I know a little; how to count to ten, how to offer tea or coffee. Yes and no, hello, goodbye. Thank you. And that's all I'll ever know, even if I try again, if I go to night classes. Because you can't learn it that way, as your own language, unless you're a kid.

But Yiayia never seems disappointed in me, never rebukes me for refusing the one thing that would have tied us together beyond a name. And I never get frustrated with our half-language, because it's only ours, and I don't have to share it with the other kids. It makes me special.

She touches the vine gently, lovingly tracing the veins on the leaves and smiles at me, nudging me with her elbow. Then she puts out a hand to help me stand. She tucks a greying hair behind her ear, and straightens her dress, black with little white dots. She's always in black, but the polka dots cheer it up, make her less like all those other little old Greek ladies in their dark clothes and sensible shoes. She taps the stick that supports the vine.

'To make little one grow strong, be steady.' She stands behind me, and puts her arms around me, linking her hands across my shoulders. I feel her warmth against my back and lean into her.

'Growing,' she says, '*oloi mazi.*'

She kisses my cheek, and gives my arm a squeeze before moving back inside with her basket full of vine leaves, ready to start cooking.

All together, she said.

Chapter Five

Nicky sat next to me on the damp grass in the garden, a freshly-rolled cigarette sitting behind his ear. He never smoked in front of our parents, although whether that was out of respect, or out of a desire to avoid a lecture, I don't know. We sat in the dark, watching as the lights flicked off from room to room, tracing our parents' movements, a countdown to the end of that awful day.

'They asleep, d'ya think?' I asked as Nicky flicked back and forth on his silver Zippo. I'd gotten it engraved for him as a twenty-first birthday present, and he was never without it. Dad said I was just encouraging bad habits. I didn't point out that my father's own silver lighter was in constant use. It wasn't engraved. So maybe that made it okay.

'Give Nina a few more minutes,' Nicky mumbled around the cigarette as he toked the flame, giving in. First toke of a terrible day never really tastes sweet, just insufficient.

'Urgh, I hate it when you call her Nina. Just call her Mum, would you?' I reached out my hand for his cigarette, and he passed it over. Quick inhale, slight splutter. Nicotine never did anything for me.

'It's her name,' Nicky shrugged.

'You call Dad 'Dad'.'

'That's because he's just Dad. Nina's not just Mum.'

I sighed, and lay back on the grass, feeling the cold soak through the hoodie I pulled on over my funeral dress. The Nirvana hoodie I'd had since forever, still warm and worn, and comforting, even though it was falling apart, bobbling with washing and wear. The cross-eyed smiley face had almost completely peeled off by that point, but I needed it, like a hug from an old friend.

'So, what now?' I asked, picking at my nails. My eyes adjusted to the dark, and Nicky's face was soft and reddish from the glow at the end of the cigarette. He looked down to the end of the garden, his sharp features jutting from his profile, the uncut hair falling in front of his eyes. He shook his head, and breathed out smoke.

'No clue.'

'You moving back home?'

'I guess so, they won't let me stay at hers. It would be *inappropriate.*' He puffed out smoke circles expertly.

'Do you want to stay there?'

'I don't know. Probably not.'

I tugged the hood up over my head to keep my ears warm, and stared at the sky. You could never see the stars in London, even in the suburbs. You thought you saw them, occasionally, usually whilst drunk or high. But it was never true. Just reflections of streetlights, and planes in the sky.

I heard the slight fizzle as Nicky stubbed out the cigarette on Dad's prize lawn. Hopefully he'd be too busy mourning to notice, but I doubted it. He'd storm into the house on Sunday demanding we file out to assess the damage with him. Or maybe her death had changed everything.

'I need to tell you something,' Nicky said quietly. 'You're not going to like it, you're going to hate me. But I need to tell someone.'

A sudden weight hung briefly in my chest before dropping into my stomach. I scrunched my eyes closed and held my breath until I had to gasp. It didn't help. I was used to this, to being the secret keeper. It was okay, it would be fine, it always was. He'd confess to me, we'd talk it down until it seemed completely unimportant, and we'd never talk about it again. I searched my brother's face for the answer. He'd relapsed, he had to have. The stress of Yiayia, of everything changing on him, he'd made a mistake, and he was sorry.

'I won't hate you,' I said, 'Tell me.'

'I just can't deal with it by myself, I need you to know, and I can't tell *them*, obviously...'

'Nicky, tell me.'

Nicky was in as small a ball as he could be, his long legs pulled close to him, his head bowed. His voice was a whisper.

'She did it on purpose.'

For once, I had nothing to say. Even thinking about how to react took so much energy. I sat up slowly, aching, and looked out at the dark outlines of the trees, the vine in the garden so like *Yiayia's,* except that ours had never managed to produce grapes.

'Don't do this Nicky.'

I heard as the sob broke, as he muffled it with his suit jacket, more crumpled than ever.

It wasn't his fault, I knew it wasn't his fault, that he didn't understand. That it had been too much to deal with. I knew from before that this was that step before the paranoia became full-blown. Soon he would tell me that they came in the night and took her away, brought her back wrong. That it was a plot, a mystery to be solved. That our parents, our family and friends, everyone was in on it, and we had to fix it. I had to believe him, he would beg, he'd cry and plead. I had to believe him, I was the only one who would listen. He would spout more and more shit, more tangled lies that made no sense, desperate for me to understand. So earnest, so truthful. It was the truth, he knew, he swore. 'When did you start using again?' I hated myself for asking. We never talked about that.

The disgusted silence almost crushed me with the weight of relief.

'Jesus Christ, Ellie. No,' he threw back, 'I was just the person who found her, who cared for her. Who do you think taught her which pills to take?'

I tried to reach for him, 'No-one's blaming you, Nicky. It was an accident. She was getting older. She was on so much medication for different things, it could have happened naturally.'

'But it didn't. She did this.'

'Why would she kill herself? Be serious,' I said, trying to emphasise the ridiculousness of the idea. But even as I said it, my mind ran through alternatives. *When was the last time I'd seen her smile, not a twitch of a heavily wrinkled mouth, but a smile? A laugh? When did she stop saying 'I alright, dear, I alright' and start saying 'I ready to go, too old now.'* That seemed like forever ago.

'Withdrawal.'

The small bathroom light flicked on upstairs, and made me jump. Dad, most likely. I had got used to the sounds of the house, the little routines no-one even noticed they had. We waited in silence until the window fell to black again. All I wanted to do was scream, stop him from telling these stupid stories. I whispered angrily.

'Withdrawal from what, Nicky? You're saying she was an addict? A pensioner with a coke habit, was that it? Or what, she wanted to see what you thought was so great about drug use, and decided to give it a go?'

My voice sounded spiteful, and all I wanted to scream was *no, no, I'm sorry, I don't mean it. But don't take her away from me again. She's gone already. Let the memories be good. Don't let me think there was something I could have done. Don't make me feel selfish for being alive, Nicky, please. Let her lie.*

Nicky looked at me briefly, slightly more together, enough to question my tone with a simple raised eyebrow, in a very 'older brother' sort of way. That was a low blow, and I was the little sister, and I should trust him. He had things to tell me. I winced and mouthed 'sorry'. He nodded and began the story.

'A few weeks ago she changed doctor, Dr Athenalios retired. The new doctor couldn't figure out what some of the prescriptions were for. One was for valium.'

He paused, waiting to see if I would interject. Or blame him for something. He carried on.

'*Yiayia* had no idea. Athenalios had given it to all the women, it was in style, the equivalent of gin. A relaxant for the stress of being a mother, a wife, a servant. A little something to make it all easier.

'The new doctor arranged to lower the dosage and take her off gradually. But once I'd translated it for her, once she knew what it was, she refused to take it. I thought, I thought I'd convinced her. I'd asked her to take it, begged her. Of all people, I knew how much it would hurt, sudden withdrawal like that. And she listened. She stroked my hair and called me a good boy. And it was good for a few weeks. Then I found her.'

He buried his head in his hands again, so much like a little boy in his big suit. I could hear his breathing, erratic, and knew it was pure force of will that let him continue.

'I should have known, when she talked about it, she looked so determined. And angry, I've never seen her so angry. She said she'd been sleepwalking through life for years. All those years when she never felt really happy, never ecstatic. Never completely in love, absolutely overwhelmed. Everything was just 'okay'. She'd spent years punishing herself, feeling guilty for never loving anyone or anything, for never smiling enough, never being happy enough. They'd taken that from her.'

I stared up at the sky, and the grass smelled beautiful and wet, and Nicky was about to cry. But when he talked again, he sounded terrifyingly calm, collected. Cold.

'There was no blood, no amateur dramatics. Just a bunch of pills, every kind she'd taken for years, with a glass of *commaderia* on the bedside table. She was just asleep, in her black dress with the daisies on it.'

His shoulders started to shake, and I strained to hear him, muffled through his coat. 'And the worst part, the worst part...there was a pot of soup on the stove that she'd made for me because she knew I was coming, knew I'd be-' his breathing quickened, 'It was still wa...s...still...warm.'

He collapsed into sobs then, weird, heavy sounds that I'd never heard from my brother. He sounded like he was choking. I reached out a hand, placed palm-up on the grass. If he needed me, he'd reach for me, I wasn't going to force him. I saw him bite his knuckles to hide the sound, and look back up to the house to see if there was a response.

'How do we tell them?' I nodded towards the dark house.

'You can't think that's a good idea, Ellie.' He dragged his cuff across his eyes, little boy again. 'Dad would go nuts.'

'Dad wouldn't believe us.'

'Exactly, and he shouldn't have to. Let them remember the good stuff. Don't take it away from them.' He stretched his arms above his head and yawned, and I suddenly felt so drained, so empty and worn, like a ragdoll, unable to hold my own head up.

'Then why did you take it away from me?' I asked in a small voice before I could stop myself.

His smile was a small twitch at the side of his mouth.

'Because you're strong, El, you can handle it. And I can't deal with it on my own. I'm really sorry, I can't. I need you to know why, if I...if I slip up.'

I wanted to hate him, but I knew I should tell him it was good, that he did the right thing coming to me. That I was glad he shared the burden with me. But, truthfully, it was just one more thing to lie about.

'It won't be for long,' he promised, a shaky smile on his face, like a little boy with his messy hair, trying to win me over.

'Why, do you plan on ever telling them?'

'No,' he sighed, 'but we just have to get through the forty days, wear black, mourn her and remember her, and then it'll be over. It gets easier to forget over time.'

'Forty days.' It was tradition for the family of the deceased to wear black, to forego drink, to mourn visibly. Nicky and Dad would not shave, and gradually begin to look rough, like they'd let themselves go. Nicky would look the way he did just before he left to go to Manchester. Dad's beard would no doubt turn grey. Everyone looked older, and worn, like they were falling apart. And that was the point. You fall apart, and on the fortieth day, you say goodbye to the person you loved, and rebuild your life without them.

I didn't do the forty days for my grandfather, I was too young to really understand what it meant. It's hard not to wear colours when you're a kid, it's like giving up being happy. But really, that's what I should do, wasn't it? Give up everything that would have made her ashamed of me. Give up drinking and drugs and sex, the one-night-friendships and two am calls to dealers. The partying, the laughing, the selfish thoughts about my stupid life. I should give up being happy for two months. I owed her that. Anything to erase how out of my fucking head I'd been whilst she'd been choking down pills for a different reason. I tried to guess exactly what I was doing when she died, but it was all a blur, like it usually was.

Forty days wasn't so hard, to be part of my heritage for once, to do what tradition dictated. It was easy enough most days not to be happy, sometimes you didn't even need to try. But this time I would do it for her. No drugging, clubbing, drinking, laughing. No happiness. For her, to honour all those years she couldn't be happy. To remember that I could turn it on again at any time, that I knew how to get all the things that would make me feel alive again. I wasn't like her. No happiness, for you, *Yiayia*, I promise.

Chapter Six

Pub. Friday night.

'Let's do shots!' I screamed across the table, 'My round!'

Lee and Mags shrugged, identical raised eyebrows, and Dex offered two thumbs up.

'Nice one bruuvaaaaa!' He followed me to the bar, miming carrying drinks. He then proceeded to mime drunkenly staggering into people and spilling this invisible tray of drinks all over them. Except he really was staggering into people. Luckily, Dex is the type of guy who can get away with that kind of shit, laugh it off with a sincere 'sorry mate!' Shake their hand and stride off leaving the accosted punter feeling like they met a real stand-up guy.

Bastard.

'What's up with you tonight?' Dex moved in closer as we elbowed our way to a stool, my hands resting on the wooden bar, sticky and wet, smelling like stale beer and afternoons at uni. Everyone seemed to be so close, cramped, and I felt like I couldn't breathe. It was too hot. I decided I didn't really like crowds unless I was out of my head. Then they just seemed like a collection of awesome people, tied together by the peculiar incidence of being in the same awesome place at the same awesome time. Awesome. But when I was just drinking, even if I was drinking a lot, it just made me want to be at home, on the sofa in my pyjamas, eating cold pizza, and watching pointless TV.

I looked up at Dex, his dark hair spiked with too much gel, his black shirt and jeans combo once again. It always seemed to be a winning look for him, if the reactions from the two girls next to us were anything. Always the way with Dex. I knew he was a massive geek, but somehow all those girls he charmed into bed never really seemed to figure it out.

'What's up with tonight, tonight?' I replied. *Don't make me talk while I'm happily hammered. That's the whole point. I don't want to do this, I don't want to do anything sober, I don't want to think. And fuck you if you ask me one damn thing about my life, because I'll blurt it out in a goddamn minute.*

I smiled at the girl behind the bar, who leaned forward to take my order. Dex's eyes wandered to her cleavage and stayed there until she turned away to get Apple Sourz or Sambuca or whatever the hell disgusting drink I just ordered.

'No seriously though,' his eyes were back on me, and he pulled me into a loose hug, irritating the people behind us queuing for the bar 'what's going on?'

Holding me close enough to be comforting, but distant enough not to ruin any offers from other women. Dex was good like that. He was confident, a pleaser. And that drew them in, always had, since we were kids on the playground, and I acted as his lawyer, his official companion. Yes, Dex will kiss you, but you only get to be his girlfriend this break-time, he's got another appointment at lunch. The same applied years later, yes, you can be his one-night stand, his screwing saviour, but I am always going to be here. I am permanent, you are just passing through.

'Tell Dex all about it,' he leant against the barstool and patted his knee.

I laughed, 'Not the night for it sweets, just a shitty couple of days. That's all.' *True enough.*

He squeezed me briefly, and then reached passed me for a shot, held it up in tribute, and then downed it. 'I'll get the chasers!' He winked, 'Seeing as I'm the only one with a real job.'

I rolled my eyes, but it was true. Dex did pretty well, managing *Ciaou Baby's,* a cafe behind Leicester Square. Open till the early hours, but making enough spare change to go drinking every weekend, buy his nice shirts, give his Dad some housekeeping money. Plus, surprisingly, he was good at it. He had that quintessentially Italian thing, he made people feel welcome. They saw his olive skin and dark eyes, standing in the entrance of *Baby's,* and thought *this is an authentic establishment, we'll be happy here.* He just had that something.

I couldn't tell him about *Yiayia.* Dex, who had known my grandmother since we were kids, and loved her. Dex, who has lost his own Nonni the year before, and would have understood exactly what I was going through, exactly what strain it put on a family when you were part of a culture like that, one that owned you, but you didn't belong to. He would have pitied me. He would have wanted to be at the funeral, to protect me, to say goodbye. He would be furious at me for not letting him pay his respects, not allowing him to be there for me. He'd always said I didn't trust him with the Big Stuff.

Yiayia used to ask about Dex all the time, she adored him. During those years he and I weren't talking I used to make up stories about him, so I had something to say when she asked. I didn't want to admit we stopped being friends, I thought she'd be disappointed. So I made up adventures, camping trips and concerts, silly jokes and the rituals we had as kids, and it was almost real for me too. Yiayia used to pat my hand, wink, and say if I couldn't marry a Greek, an Italian was a good second choice. 'Anything but an Englishman, *kori*, they have no fire.'

Dexter was by then in full-on flirtation mode with the barmaid, who although she was having none of it, had softened slightly. I elbowed him in the ribs.

'Don't get jealous, princess.' He kissed my cheek, 'I'll get to you.'

I was used to those kind of remarks by then, it was our little game. But it was so bloody tiring. The constant banter took so much energy, and I was getting tired of worrying about what I said, how I said it, if I sounded jealous. Dex had a way of making me feel fifteen again, and I hated it.

'Hey, what happened to Clone Boy, the other night at Fabric?'

'Clone Boy?' I raised my voice, suddenly tired of having to shout to be heard every weekend.

'The one who was off his head, you guys were hugging all night, getting excited about the space-time continuum, or some bollocks.' He raised his eyebrows, which he didn't have a right to. Fine, Dex never did drugs, but he got more wasted on alcohol than anyone I knew. If he remembered the night before, he considered it a dud. If it didn't end with a shag, passing out and then vomiting a few hours later, all that money he'd spent on alcohol hadn't done its job. The memory loss moments scared me, but for him, it was what he aimed for. Proof of a good night.

I shrugged, 'That could have been any of them.' *Daniel*. Daniel, who had green curtains and played the guitar badly. Who believed in life on other planets, and often wondered if there were versions of him in alternate universes that could juggle, or speak French.

33

'They all look the same, that's why,' he paused and took a gulp from a fresh pint, spilling half down him, 'In fact, they all look like me.'

He looked at me sideways and grinned like he'd hoped I'd get embarrassed. 'Still not over it, love?'

He nudged me too hard and spilled his drink again. Idiot.

To be fair, they *did* all look like Dex. More beautiful versions of Dex. Less lanky, taller, stronger, lighter eyes and wider smiles. Dex two-point-ones and twos and threes, all the way up to double digits. He'd probably worked that out for himself, though.

I sighed, 'Just because I have a type doesn't mean I have good taste.'

I kissed him on the mouth, briefly but firmly, pulling back to say 'good luck getting with the barmaid now. Toodles!'

I grabbed the shots and let him follow with the tray of drinks. He'd probably want to take The Scenic Route, as he called it. Scoping out his Friday night conquest. We weren't that different in many respects, our flaw was the same, essentially. We needed strangers. Dex needed to fuck them and throw them away. Get what he wanted and move on, stay free. I wanted to get high with them, learn their stories. Hold their hands whilst they chatted shit about their feelings and memories. Capture the little pieces of themselves they never showed anyone else. Only then I could tell them my secrets at some ridiculous time in the morning, when they felt like they knew me better than anyone in the world, and I would never see them again.

I hugged Lee from behind as I approached her, as always, when drunk or otherwise, overwhelmed by how much I loved her. She was nursing her glass of white, laughing at Magda's story about accidentally living in an opium den in Cambridge. I'd heard it before, but it was nice to laugh along without listening. Lee was all about the real stuff, she would have been the person to tell. She would have rubbed a hand through her cropped blond hair, her green eyes would have widened and she'd have said 'Oh darling, I'm so sorry.' Then it would be a toss-up as to whether she enveloped me in a incense-scented bear hug, or reached for the polka dot cookie jar, which had helped us through many a crisis.

She would be sympathetic, let me mourn and moan until I was sick of my own voice and my own life, and would feel terrified about how much I'd revealed. Like I was suddenly naked, and everyone could see right through me, and use it against me. Lee never would, but I still got that sick feeling in my stomach when I told anyone about my family, or the things I remembered. Even memories that weren't bad, they were mine, they weren't for anyone else. Unless I was fucked, and they were strangers, and then they could have them, add them to their own stories, to be forgotten in the morning, just like mine.

I should have told Lee. But I couldn't bear to drag anyone down with one more meaningless bit of reality. Not when we could go on drinking and laughing and living. I'd already broken my promise, so why not carry on having a good time? And maybe later I could score something in the girls' toilet at the back of the pub, or from some skeezy fucker outside the tube station. And at the very least I could share a joint with a beautiful boy, sitting on a worn-out sofa in a student house, whilst he held my hand and talked about politics, or something else that I would half-listen to, and he would cease to believe in five years or so anyway.

That was why I loved ecstasy, the safety of it. The chemical equivalent of that moment in a conversation when you should say 'I have a boyfriend'. The platonic pill. They are physically unable to try anything with you, they may want you, but they'll settle for friends. Impotence in trade for understanding. But they don't stop touching you, holding your hand, stroking your hair, telling you you're lovely. Because you've got a 'connection'. The perfect one-night-friendship.

And there was a dark haired boy across the room with a dull checked shirt and wire rimmed glasses who was smiling like he knew all about me. Like he wanted to be my one-night-friend.

'And Ellie scores again!' Magda sang out, 'Ding ding ding, we have a winner!'

'Oh calm down, I bought you a drink didn't I? Be nice!' I stuck out my tongue and didn't look at the boy again, trying to be good. Trying to be someone Yiayia would be proud of. Proper, prim, a sense of decorum. And what was the point of a one night friend with no drugs, anyway? Although, I'd already started drinking. Break one rule, break them all? 'Maybe I don't want to be stared at.'

'Smiled at,' Lee corrected.

'Such a charismatic and popular woman, ladies and gentlemen,' Dex announced, 'If only they knew the real her...'

'Jealous, darling?' I fluttered my lashes, eager to change the subject from dark-haired boys. I wasn't on anything, I was just slightly drunk, and that wasn't enough for it to be normal. I only needed a boy when I knew he was just as out of it as me. And I wasn't out of it at all.

'For you, my darling,' Dex started, his assumed Italian accent cheesy and over the top. He knelt on the floor, amongst the beer spills and crushed crisps. It was his party piece.

36

'My heart, my life's meaning, for you, I would climb to the moon! And tie a balloon, to the nearest baboon, for you! I would shoot a buffoon, at noon, and...draw a cartoon for you! I would hit a loon, and a goon, and uh,' he trailed off and shrugged, 'buy you some flowers or something.'

We applauded, and some people around us looked over.

'Five out of ten,' Mags shrugged, 'not as good as the one about the bees from Kathmandu.'

'I give seven,' Lee smiled, 'because I like the idea of a balloon on the moon.' She sipped her wine thoughtfully. 'But other than that, utter bollocks.'

'That's what they tell me,' Dex laughed.

I allowed myself to fade into the background as I didn't listen to Mags flirting with Dex, Lee's laughter at another crazy story. Let the background grow fuzzy, like a badly tuned television, static. I stared from behind my eyes into the soft glow of the pub, so that all the moving, talking, living bodies just became blurs of pink and olive and brown. And when I focused, the boy across the pub in the checked shirt was looking at me. Looked exactly like a one-night-friend waiting to happen. But I wouldn't talk to him. Couldn't. Not sober. Not drug-free. Never.

'Hey,' Lee nudged me, and spoke quietly, watching as Dex and Mags started another debate, their hands moving about wildly, 'whatever's bothering you, we'll talk this week, yes? I'll make brownies.'

'Chocolate fudge?'

'With sprinkles!' She winked, and reached one arm around me.

'You have no idea how lucky I am to know you,' I rested my head against hers.

'Well then, you better listen when I tell you a boy over there wants your attention. And I think you should go over there.' She grinned, impish, with dimples in her cheeks. 'And maybe leave the usual bullshit out of it.'

I looked over again, and Dex two-point-whatever raised a hand in greeting. I wasn't going, if only for the fact that it was crowded, and loud, and I couldn't bear to talk to anyone.

'Never underestimate the feel-good factor of a good crush,' Lee nodded, sage-like, 'Now get your cute behind over there.' She gave me a slight push, and Magda clapped her hands. Dex looked at me like he knew I'd never do it. Like he was daring me.

'Someone chicken?' He stage whispered, grin in place.

I growled and stood up, ready to prove him wrong. Instead, I thought perhaps I'd leave. That'd show him, son of a bitch. I walked towards the door, and stopped, unsure.

Then the alcohol-induced fog cleared, and a dark-haired guy in a checked shirt was staring at me. Up close. Daniel. Daniel standing in my favourite pub, laughing at me for being so goddamn blind. Fucking ugly glasses as camouflage.

'So, had the funeral yet?' He shouted over the music, hands in pockets, voice as light as if he was asking about the weather, enquiring as to the health of my mother. Proper gent.

'Feel like starting with a more normal question?' I bit back.

'Okay, here's a normal question. How would you feel if you spent all night telling someone your secrets, all morning and afternoon holding them, and then they disappeared?' That half-twitch of a smile again.

'You've got my number.'

'I called it, you didn't answer,' he sighed, 'and let's face it Ellie, you were never going to, were you?'

I placed my hands on my hips, straightened my back. I could have stood there, staring at my shoes, feeling guilty, but why should I? I looked across the room to Lee, who was giving me a thumbs up, and Dex and Mags who were blowing kisses. Best way not to feel guilty? Get mad.

'I'm sorry, did we get married? I thought we spent a night on drugs, and then I woke up and found out my grandmother was dead. I didn't realise that created a committed relationship. Is there some sort of ruling, about girls you let into your flat or something? Are we not allowed to leave without a minimum number of dates?'

'Ellie-'

'Stop saying my name! I'm sorry I didn't answer the phone. I was kind of busy with a funeral, and my family, and keeping everyone else's bloody secrets!'

He stepped forward, and I had to tilt my neck back to look at him. Tall.

'I had a good time with you,' he smiled, ignoring my outburst, and I felt my chest constrict, just a little. My tongue itched and my fingers twitched. I was not drunk enough for other people.

There were rules, post-comedown decorum. You meet the person you got fucked with, days, weeks, months later, at a club, because they do the circuit the same way you do. And you're both fucked again, and you embrace each other like old friends, because you had that one night, and it was brilliant. You introduce this person to your friends as a legend, and that's it. You hug and laugh, high five. Maybe, if you're lucky, they've got a contact for the night, and you can get an eighth of something, or a gram of something else. Maybe they're already fucked and willing to share.

But if you do it sober you realise you're just strangers pretending to be friends.

'What do you want, exactly?'

'It's really simple, Ellie, nothing weird,' he radiated goodwill like a fucking Christmas tree, 'I just want to get to know you.'

I wanted to tell him that he'd be disappointed. That I didn't want him to know me, I didn't need him or anyone. I just wanted to be with my friends, and go home and not think about my grandmother, or how my father wasn't talking, and Nicky wouldn't leave his room, and me and Mum sat eating dinner alone most nights. I wanted to tell him to fuck off, stop pretending he cared about some girl who was just passing through. Tell him to stop being such a child about it, grow up, move on.

But there was an itching in my stomach as I remembered his cold hands, warm smile, and how calm I felt in the little white room with the green curtains.

'Okay,' I said.

Chapter Seven

The colours faded from her gradually. In almost all my memories, she's wearing black. Black smock dresses that wave as she hobbles along. When I look through the photo albums, it seems like it happened little by little over the years. Navy blues and forest greens, greys and browns down to black, day in, day out, forever more. The photos from when she's young are in black and white, so I pretend that she's wearing these beautiful bright colours, that people pass by her and notice the girl with the ocean blue dress, or the red jumper with that lace collar. But it's hard to imagine her in anything but dark clothing. Occasionally she wears a black dress with little white flowers dotted all over. I call it her daisy dress. I like to think she wears it when she's happy.

There's one Christmas I remember when she wears this beautiful red dress, tucking up the ruffly sleeves as she carves the turkey, her dark hair curling around her face and I think she's so so pretty, and I hope one day I look like her. Everyone tells me I already do. Although when I think about it, it was more plum or maroon, dark, always dark. And really, I'm not remembering that Christmas, but the homemade video that my uncle took on the video camera he got that year. He dropped the camera, Yiayia jumped and burnt her hand. Mum and Dad got into an argument before dessert, and we drove home in silence to play with our toys, wondering why happiness never lasted a whole day, even at Christmas. Maybe that was why she wore black. Safer, doesn't get anyone's hopes up.

I always dress in bright colours when we go to Yiayia's, because the whole place is dark and old. Dark purple sofa, and the heavy curtains and the matted animal fur rug where we play, now threadbare from our games.

Crocheted blankets with holes in, and a big, shiny black vase on the floor with imitation peacock feathers poking out the top. Yiayia calls the peacock tails 'evil eyes' and they match the blue glass talismans that hang in the kitchen, the only light part of the house. Her fingers graze the feathers as she walks past, and I hear her whisper what might be prayers.

I ask my parents why Yiayia always wears black. Mama says it happens to old Greek ladies, that eventually, at their age, they go to so many funerals that they just carry on wearing black. By the time they reach the end of the forty days of mourning, another one's dropped. Dad congratulates her on phrasing it so delicately. She tolls her eyes and tells me it means Yiayia is always missing someone, always mourning.

Nicky asks Yiayia directly, and though he asks in Greek, she answers in English, like it's something I need to know too.

'To remember, *lavendi,* that why I wear. Black to show you sad. To remember them all.'

She strokes his hair, calls him a good boy, and I run off to play on the swing in the garden, whilst Nicky stays to talk to her in their language. Black to remember, show your sorrow, prove your loyalty. Always in mourning, my grandmother, always awaiting the next death.

Chapter Eight

It spurted hot and wet over my hand as he sighed. I held my breath and reached for the tissues to the far side of the desk, always to hand. I never looked at Paul, never looked at anything except the Rothko print on the wall, red and angry. Sometimes I got squeamish, let go of him at the last minute, and it ended up on the underside of his desk. Luckily I never had to clean his office for real, although I suppose that's what his cover story was. I got up slowly, the carpet making shapes in my knees. He let out this pathetic little whimper and said my name. I hated when he said my name.

'Well, I guess I'll be off,' my voice came from somewhere outside of me. I wasn't me, I was just some cleaner at an Art Gallery. I didn't look Paul in the eye, but focused on his chin. His wobbling, oily chin, with a few dark hairs and open pores, warbling and puffing as he calmed himself.

'Yes, well, you...You're-' he paused, his face pink and shining, his rounded body bouncing in his seat as he tucked himself back into his trousers, 'you're a very talented girl, Ellie. You'll go far.'

He always said that, but it always felt like a question. How far will you go Ellie?

It was always six fifteen, on the dot, Friday afternoon. I looked down at my watch, six twenty three. Soon enough he'd blow before I'd even got through the door.

I paused with my hand on the door handle, and turned on my heel, forcing myself to look into his little squinty eyes, so full of satisfaction. I felt a wave of disgust that was easier to deal with when I was on something, anything. Only a few hours to go until Friday night and whatever I

43

could find. The bastard had become part of my routine. Except I wasn't doing that anymore. The drugs, that is. Paul however, was an unfortunate necessity.

'Paul?'

'Yes, Ellie?' I hated when he said my name.

'Do you think you've got some time next week to have a look at some of my work? A few exhibition pieces.' I looked down at the floor, then up at the ceiling.

'Why, of course! I'd love that, you're so talented, I'd love to see what you're up to!' He sounded pleased I'd asked, proud of me.

Paul had been saying that since I started, that I was a 'great talent', they needed 'bright young creatives' like me. That my generation was going to change the world. It just highlighted how old he was. I didn't know his age exactly, I judged him by the pinstripe suit, the overwhelming cologne he bathed in. The way his eyes traced the outline of any woman in her twenties.

'It's just last time, you were too busy,' I smiled past him, 'I just want to make sure I don't take up your time.'

'You will have my full attention, I promise.' He nodded, 'Now, run along.' He put on his little glasses and I closed the door behind me, leaning against it briefly. I walked down the corridor, hand held out to the side, not touching anything. I walked into the first floor ladies bathroom, and held my hair back with my other hand as I tried to be sick. Nothing but a few sharp hacks, air and spit. I washed my hands and stared into the mirror. Drawn, pale, angry girl. Black clothes, long lank hair that weighed her down.

Paul *was* going to see my work. He was going to see I had talent, and recommend me to the smaller gallery owners. He was going to keep his ears open for me. And when I finally had an exhibition, a gallery contract, Paul would be one of those stories from my past. A symbol of what I would go through for my art, that my bohemian friends would laugh about over canapes and champagne. *Oh god, we've all been there darling,* they'd laugh. And all I would do was paint all day, and drink all night. Take pills and smile and paint how beautiful it was. That would be my life. And it would be worth it.

Dad was not going to win, I thought grimly as I dragged the grey mop across the floor. I got to sweep and wash beneath Rothkos, Picassos, Modiglianis. I got to see and touch these creations when no-one else was around. I got to pretend they were mine. And I would get my work on those walls, I would do anything. If I needed to wank off a gallery official, pay off an agent, beg, plead and cry myself to sleep every night, I would be a real artist. Dad was standing in the shadows, waiting for me to fail, waiting for me to come home, head bowed, apologising for being so naive. To start a law conversion course, and try one last time to make him proud.

I ran my fingers across the paintings, glaring at the security camera flashing red at me. I got to be so close to that world, but not a part of it. And Dad had no idea how far I'd go to prove him wrong. I twitched my mouth up at the corners. Being numb was an advantage with Paul. It wasn't even really harrowing anymore. Just like another boring part of my cleaning job, like tugging on the hoover nozzle or wiping down the railings. I preferred it, in fact, to making chirpy conversation with the ladies in the cafeteria. At least it was honest.

They didn't say I'd be a cleaner, they said I'd be 'gaining valuable experience'. Paul didn't say I'd be his right-hand woman, he said I'd 'have opportunities unavailable to other interns'. And each time, huff and puff, and out with the tissues. Scared of making a mess, unable to colour inside the lines. I didn't say 'I'm a cleaner who wanks off a man who disgusts me', I said 'I'm working at an art gallery in Pimlico at the moment.' It's all about promotion, self-perception, presentation.

That's art, babe.

Chapter Nine

Another Saturday afternoon in Camden market, and my head was killing me. I'd stayed off the drugs, just as I'd planned. But I'd been out with Dex, and there was no way to deal with a Friday night with Dex without drinking. I couldn't match him drink for drink, but if I was ridiculous enough, charming and hilarious enough, I could stop him abandoning me in the club for another nameless bimbo. He probably did fit in a shag whilst I queued for the toilets, but he went home with me. He even held my hair back while I threw up. Which then made him throw up. True friendship.

And even though I was used to the Saturday morning comedown, the Saturday morning hangover was somehow much worse. I could feel the vodka seeping from my pores, and it was weirdly sunny, but cold. I pulled on my half-broken sunglasses, pulled my scarf around me and sat on Mags' little stool that she bought for me after I'd moaned about standing around for hours every weekend. Everything in the market was too colourful, too loud, smelled too exotic. Too many people nudging each other, bumping into things, bartering, trading germs, stories, money. On mornings like that it freaks me out how many people have touched the coins they hand over, how many twenty pounds have been used to snort stuff. I feel like there's fluids on everything, and it makes me nauseous.

It's Magda's stall, her living, but she helped me out when I first started trying to flog stuff. It was too expensive to get my own plot in Camden, so when I came home from uni, she used to flog my paintings over the summer. Since I graduated, there hadn't been much painting, what with working at the gallery. Just my final pieces, proof of four years spent studying. Honing my craft, apparently. But

my work felt fusty and irrelevant. Completely incapable
of showing who I was, what I could do. So, for the time
being, I was making jewellery for Mags to sell. Stuff that
complemented her swirly skirts, geometric prints, tie dye
t-shirts. Mostly little beaded bracelets, ceramic earrings.
Plastic necklaces that looked like a three year old could
have made them. They went down well with the Japanese
tourists. I started painting mini Hello Kitty symbols on
everything and realised that meant I could charge an
extra pound. It was hardly real 'art', but it was work. And
anything that got me closer to being a paid artist was
worth it.

Besides, it was just Saturday afternoons, and Sundays.
And I hated Sundays. I'd rather be anywhere than at
home on a Sunday. It's a day that encourages arguments,
usually out of boredom. So, rain or shine, or usually in
between, I sat on an uncomfortable stool for five hours,
bought some chinese food, perused the second hand
bookshop, and went home.

Mags was off chatting to Tony, the old punk who ran the
t-shirt stall opposite. Everything was Metallica and Iron
Maiden. The funny thing was, Tony, with his bleach
blond mohawk, leather jacket and Doc Martins, hated
rock music. He especially hated Metallica. He'd mellowed
over time. Apparently he listened to folk. But it's
Camden; image is everything. I used to step out of the
tube at Camden Town and at once, feel at home. Lately, it
had felt like I just wasn't cool enough to be there
anymore. I wasn't marketable, I didn't have a brand, an
image. I was just me, the unemployed art graduate who
made shitty jewellery and overcharged for it.

But I enjoyed making the shitty jewellery, enjoyed
threading the tiny beads onto the thin bits of string, using
bits I'd found around the house, smashing up old teacups

from charity shops, filing them down and making pendants. It was therapeutic. It wouldn't get me an exhibition, but it was better than being on the dole because you were overqualified to work in a supermarket, like every other graduate I knew.

The sun made my face feel greasy, and I wiped at my nose, irritable. I knew, once I got into one of those moods, I wouldn't get out. The crowds, the people yelling, getting stuck walking behind slow tourists who wouldn't move out of the fucking way. Give in to the bad mood, do anything to feel better. So, I shuffled my stool back a bit, hunched over and rolled a mini joint.

Okay, so it was stupid, really stupid. But I was hungover, and I knew it would help. It wasn't like I was going to enjoy it. But as soon as I sparked it, took the first deep inhale and the stale aftertaste, every muscle in my body released, and I thought *Yes, God yes*.

Release.

'Hey,' a surprised voice called out, and I jumped, my heart pounding in my throat. Plain clothes police. Stupid fucking girl. Stupid. I stubbed the joint out on the stool and dropped it to the floor. And then I looked up, and it was Daniel.

I rolled my eyes and picked up the joint, blowing the end to remove ash before putting it in my coat pocket.

'What are you, my conscience? Because, believe me, I know I'm doing wrong.' I twitched my mouth in irritation. He looked different, yet again. When I met him in the club that night, he'd had one of those Human Traffic 'Junglist' t-shirts on, that's what we started talking about. And then at the pub, with those wire rimmed glasses. And then here, in Camden, in the market. The glasses were sitting in the front pocket of a severely worn-out shirt, faded. It used to be red, I assumed. His jeans

49

were torn, threads trailing at the bottom, and his Converse were greying. He looked like a tired little dog, in need of a tidying up, a bit of affection. His smile was wry. I always felt like he was on the verge of mocking me, and it made my stomach prickle.

'So, you work here?' He seemed shocked, so perhaps I'd lied to him that night after all. Then again, after conversations about alternate realities and whether brown M'n'Ms taste more chocolatey than the other colours, what's a conversation about a job? Your job is probably the least personal thing you can talk about.

'Only at the weekend. I work in a gallery in Pimlico during the week.' I said, daring him to be condescending. I assumed that posh London edge to my voice that only happens when you're an insecure girl who needs to prove herself. I'd convinced people I went to private school in Kensington, and it had its advantages when dealing with Art People. I hated the way it sounded.

'Wow, an artist,' he paused, 'they pay you to work at the gallery, like a curator?'

'Not...exactly.' I felt my face flush, and looked past him to the Japanese tourists approaching. Target Market. I gestured for Daniel to move in closer and out of the way. Weekends were the only time I made any money, after all. Couldn't sacrifice that for a conversation with a boy who had made me feel guilty about running out on him, and then hadn't even called me afterwards.

'Work experience?'

'Internship.'

'Ah, that's what they're calling it, are they?' His mouth twitched up at the corners, and I saw as Madga caught my eye, gesturing to Daniel, head tilted to the side in question. I shook my head to let her know there was no trouble. I smiled tightly at the Japanese girls, and turned back to the judgemental bastard.

'Well excuse me if dreams don't come easy. It's a recession and I'm trying. That's better than shooting everyone else down.'

'What's twisted your knickers?'

I rolled my eyes, 'Nothing. And don't talk about my knickers. They, like my job, are none of your business.'

He held up his hands and stepped back. 'And there's the hostility we all know and love. What happened, I thought we'd got to friendly pastures in the pub?'

I crossed my arms and tapped my foot, waiting for him to get there himself.

'Ellie, didn't you agree to let me get to know you?' He sounded like a smug school teacher, and that itching in my stomach turned into a throbbing in my fingertips. Why didn't I get the hell out like I always did? I looked down at my black jeans, black trainers, black scarf. Right, so the bastard had capitalised on my grief.

'Yes, I did.' I stated tightly, 'A week and a half ago.'

'Right...' he suddenly looked wary, like I was leading him down a path, down to a mousetrap to snap his neck.

'Oh jeez!' I snapped, and stamped my foot, instantly feeling stupid and childish. 'A week and a half ago?'

'I didn't call! Right! That's it!' He clicked his fingers, 'You're mad because I didn't call?' He smiled and his head tilted, 'I'm touched, Ellie, I thought you wanted nothing to do with me.'

I wanted to scream, 'why does everything have to be a bloody game? You win, okay. Fine, you talked me round, and I had decided I wouldn't throw myself off Suicide

Bridge if you called me. And then you didn't bother, and I had time to remember that I want to be alone. Cheers.'

He moved forward slowly in that way he had, closing in, gradually swinging into your personal space until you didn't mind that he was there at all.

'I'm sorry I didn't call. I wanted to give you time to miss me,' his voice dropped, 'evidently it worked.'

The Japanese girls hovered, holding up their trinkets and I smiled, feeling like I was grimacing, getting little paper bags and taking their money. I focused solely on this for the whole sixty seconds it took, and spared Daniel a glance. 'You know, I liked you better high. You were a lot less work.'

'Says the girl smoking a joint in public.' That smile was starting to get me.

'Again, I don't need you to be my Jimeny Cricket, thank you.' I smiled at a bunch of teenage girls, decked out in dark hoodies, their limp hair and pimpled skin. I used to be one of them, angry girls who took solace in music. I understood them. I still watched to make sure they didn't steal anything.

'I'm not your conscience, I'm your guardian angel, little girl,' Daniel said in a funny voice, and then said matter-of-factly, 'and I don't buy this angry girl routine for a minute.'

'Free country,' I shrugged, 'See you around, I guess.'

He didn't budge, just stood there, too close to me. His dark hair was standing up on end, and he kept his hands in his pockets as people moved around us, flitting from stall to stall. He stopped smiling, and just looked at me, daring me to push him, to make him move.

'Go.' I crossed my arms.

'Nope.'

'*Please*, go,' I said through gritted teeth.

'You just said it's a free country.'

I made a noise of frustration, and dragged a hand down my face, 'Why are you trying to annoy me?'

'I'm not leaving, because obviously, this is fate.'

'This is an unlucky occurrence, one that I'm trying to remedy by getting you to leave!'

'Oh Miss Angry Pants doesn't believe in fate, how surprising,' he rolled his eyes, 'how long have you worked in the market Ellie?'

'On and off for the last few years, but I don't see what-'

'I have worked on the high street for the last four years.'

'So?'

'So, we never met before! And when we did meet, it was at a time when you needed someone. And then we meet here, where we must have walked past each other a thousand times!' His eyes were wide, and his tone a little too dramatic for my taste. Excited child, with his wild hair and hopeful expression.

'You're doing this just to piss me off, aren't you?'

He grinned, 'A little, but it *is* a bit weird.'

'Where do you work then?'

He pointed across the market, 'You know Eclipse?'

'You're a tattoo artist?' I scoffed, 'you don't look like a tattoo artist.'

'Well, sorry for breaking convention, I guess.' He shrugged, and patted around his pockets like an old man who'd lost his reading glasses. He handed over a business card. Daniel Monroe. I'd never seen a business card like that, coffee stained and crumpled, with nothing more than an email address.

'So, you're an artist.'

He started thumbing through the jewellery on the table, touching everything, getting the feel of it. I remembered that from our night together; he had to touch everything to understand it. He picked up a bracelet of tanned leather strings intertwining to link up to a central blue piece of glass, with a centre of white paint, and a dark blue circle inside it.

'What is this?'

'It's an evil eye,' I shrugged 'I think it's meant to stop curses from your enemies, but my...my grandmother always said it would protect us from the Turks.'

He raised an eyebrow, thumbing the gloss of the glass.

'It's Cypriot history,' I felt awkward talking about it, like I was an impostor talking about a culture that wasn't mine 'but I never got why they sell them on both sides of the divide, the Greeks think it'll protect them from the Turks, the Turks think it will protect them from the Greeks.'

'Then why did you make something with it in?'

I shrugged again, 'there's something beautiful and scary about waiting for someone to curse you. You've bought it because you're expecting the worst, you know? A little bit of nonsense protection, that's all.'

I rubbed my arms, feeling stupid. I liked it because it was something she told me about, because when we went to her house, they hung in the window like sun catchers, that beautiful blue glass reflecting in the afternoon sun, the stark white centre somehow unsettling. The kitchen glowed like we were at the seaside, sun bouncing off blue.

They made Yiayia feel safe, and I never once wondered who she thought had cursed her.

'How much is it?' Daniel asked.

'You don't have to-'

'I like it,' he smiled, meeting my eyes, 'besides, it can only help. Wouldn't put it past you to curse me.'

'Just take it,' I shook my head and became exasperated with him, and myself. That was why I never dated, obviously. Too much bloody effort. Banter was exhausting.

'Nope, that's bad business. How about...instead of paying you for it, I take you for food? Dodgy Chinese in the market?'

I felt my mouth twitch, 'depends, one on the high street, or one next to the ice cream place?'

'Blasphemy! The one on the new corner, under that weird glass roof.'

'Ah, so you've fallen to the consumer-driven destruction of our market. Vile betrayer.'

'Well, I can appreciate them putting a roof over a bunch of stalls so I don't get soaked in winter. But besides that, I'm right there with you. Want to discuss it over noodles?'

There's very few times when you actually recognise a turning point. That some small choice could make a difference to how you live your life. That eating noodles with a strange boy instead of sharing a packet of crisps with Mags would lead somewhere. I could have turned away, gone back to Dex and his bimbos, and Mags' stories, and Lee's cookie comfort. Or I could let some crazy frustrating stranger start something with me, and feel a little loved for a while, readying myself for the moment he realised I was too much work.

'Okay, but this doesn't mean-'

'That you think there's anything appealing about me, trust me, I've got that. Come on, take a chance.'

'Mags!' I shouted over, 'I'm taking my break.'

She tilted her head to the side and widened her eyes at Daniel.

'Have fun, lovebirds!'

'Guess she needs an evil eye, too,' Daniel said as we walked away.

Chapter Ten

It's Easter Sunday, and we've gone to the grandparents' house to break eggs. We went to church on the Friday night, walked around the streets with our candles lit in mourning. Nicky said we had to be sad for Baby Jesus, but I think he was joking. All I know is they sing hymns, these scary ranging voices that start dark and deep and end up high and wailing.

The church looked beautiful, gold and glowing with hundreds of candles, all these dark people with red faces, sweating, the little old ladies puffing away at the heat of the flames. Nicky made the sign of the cross with everyone else, and I copied him a second later. Me and Gali sighed at each other, bored, waiting for the part where everyone walks around outside, trying to keep their candles lit. If the candle goes out, you light it off someone else. I like that part, it's like sharing with strangers. Little ladies hobble over to cover your candle, steal your light. Yiayia looked over at us and winked. Pappou didn't come to church, and I don't know why, he's the most religious one. He used to make us all go to Sunday service when we were kids. Me and Gali would play noughts and crosses, or hangman. He still hasn't forgiven my parents for not sending me to Greek school.

After the cold walk in the dark, we drove back to Yiayia's house. Nicky managed to keep his flame alight inside the car, and we marked the doorway with wax. It's good luck, or something. By this point, I've stopped asking why we do stuff, because the answer is always that 'we're Greek'.

That's why we paint boiled eggs bright colours, heavy reds and blues, and crack them on Sunday morning. Whichever ones don't break, we keep in a cabinet at home. Pappou says if you keep them a hundred years, the yolk of the egg turns into a diamond. But we won't be alive in a hundred years, so I won't know if he's lying.

'*Ade*, Elena! *Kori,* don't want soup get cold, no?' Yiayia gestures for me to come into the kitchen, where Nicky and Gali are already sitting at the bench in the kitchen. They've already drained a bowl of soup each. The kitchen has a blue glow, and I'm not sure I even feel like eating soup yet, it's still Sunday morning. But it's tradition.

'You started without me?' They shrug.

'You snooze, you lose,' Nicky grins, and refills his soup bowl from the pot on the table, tearing at the boiled chicken on the side and dropping the shreds into his bowl, old china with a floral pattern.

'Oh hello!' My Pappou walks through and walks to the big chair at the end of the long table, patting us each on the head, 'having *soupa*, are we?'

Sometimes, he's this sweet little old man, and sometimes he seems so mean and angry and from a completely different planet. Today, he's happy.

'Eleni, *thelo soupa!*' He yells, and my Yiayia comes in to serve his soup. Times like this, I get angry at him, for not getting up and doing it himself, even though I know that's just the way it is. My Dad and Nicky are the same, it's always that way, even if it's not fair. Men eat first, women serve and eat last. Me and Mum cook together, now I'm a bit older, and Nicky and Dad eat at the table, and then we eat together, usually because ours has gotten cold by then. I bet Mum's glad she had a girl, otherwise she'd be eating alone.

Pappou reaches over to the main pot on the table and adds more salt before he even tries it. He always does that, and Mum always mutters stuff about heart attack statistics. Yiayia puts the bowl and spoon in front of him, retreating immediately.

'Not this one,' he hands the spoon back, and I think I see her roll her eyes before handing him a bigger one, and exiting the room. He sucks on his food loudly, the way old people do, dribbling a little. I don't like watching him eat. He picks at the bones of the chicken, licking his fingers and chewing on the bits of cartilage until I hear them crack against his teeth.

'So, girls, you're taking the home economics?' He always asks us this question, and at first we used to tell him there was no home economics, only cookery, but we stopped fighting.

'Yes, Pappou.' We chorus. Nicky sniggers.

'Only way you find a good husband girls,' he nods, 'no-one wants a useless wife.' His eyes flick to the doorframe, and he wipes his mouth on his shirt cuff, leaving a greasy smear.

We laugh about it when we leave the room, me and Gali and Nicky, when we go to sit under the big table in the main room, on the floor with the big furry rug. We sit and whisper and laugh. Home economics! We'll continue to laugh about that in years to come, every time we fail a test, or get detention, we'll say 'at least we've got home economics!' I decide I don't want to get married if it means I have to have cold soup for the rest of my life.

Yiayia's shuffling feet slowly come into vision, swollen, with her little blue slippers. She bends down with surprising ease, lifting the fruit bowl from atop the table, and holds it out to us, her wide smile in place.

'You like? More? You take!' We take an apple each and she smiles like we've done something wonderful. The rule when she offers so much food is to say 'no' three times.

After that, you have to take it. She just loves to give us stuff, offering people things is most of her English vocabulary. She can't stand seeing us empty handed. And she always offers more than three times.

We sit and listen as the adults talk, commenting on the TV, sometimes in English, sometimes in Greek. The more interesting visits are when we get the photo albums out, see them all so young, see if we look like our parents. My Dad quizzes my grandparents on every single person in the photos. I used to think he did it to make conversation, but Nicky says he's checking to see they've still got their marbles.

Eventually, after a prolonged period of silence, when Yiayia offers everybody more soup, more fruit, sweets, olives and Greek coffee, they stand up to go. My parents leave first, getting the car started as we say goodbye.

Pappou moves slowly, rising from his armchair, his whiskers scratching us as he kisses on both cheeks, rattling around his pockets for a five pound note for each of us. He then stands back, smiles and delivers his personal catch phrase.

'I don't like you,' he says, 'but I love you!'

He almost falls back into his armchair, and directly returns his attention to the television, waving cheerfully. Yiayia waits at the front door, kissing us each again. Her skin is soft, but her grip is tighter. She nods her head towards her husband in the living room.

'Silly billy pussycat!' She smiles, and hands us each another fiver that she's been hiding in her apron.

She waves from the front door as we run out to the car, suddenly blinded by how light it is outside, how little of it gets into that house. The only light is in the kitchen, where her evil eyes hang in the window, catching rays and reflecting blue everywhere. Everything else is dark and comforting and night-like, blocking out reality. A different world, outside time.

We don't say much in the car, us kids, occasionally glancing at each other. Our grandfather's catchphrase tends to have that effect, dulling us down, quieting us. Like we've been told off, or told we're not good enough. Something that just makes us feel blue.

We drop Gali home, and when we get to our house, Nicky goes straight to his room as he always does, whilst me and Mum sit eating our way through the bag of fruit Yiayia gave us. Grapes and lychees. I don't like the lychees. They taste good, but have the consistency of eyes. That's what Pappou always calls them. Babies' eyes.

My father is lying on the floor, watching TV or asleep, I can't tell, when Mum nudges me.

'He said it again, didn't he, Pappou?'

I shrug, look back at the television, feeling myself get a little weepy.

'It's okay to be upset, it's a bit of a mean thing to say.' She says softly, wrapping an arm around me, her red hair tickling my neck. I shake my head, setting my jaw against getting crying.

'Let me ask you something, Ellie-mou. Do you love Pappou?'

I roll my eyes at her, 'Well, it's not like I have a choice, do I? He's family.'

My father, in one of his mystical moments, gets up, places a hand on my head, and says 'I'm very proud of you Elena,' before walking out of the room. I turn to look at my mother, bemused and she just shrugs.

'I don't like him though.' I say, disgruntled, crossing my arms over a cushion, hugging it to me.

'Well that's alright, he doesn't like you either!' She sticks her tongue out at me, and I can't help but laugh. We sit for a moment in silence.

'He's just...' my mother starts, but can't seem to find the words.

'Whatever,' I shrug, and decide that nothing he says will upset me again.

Chapter Eleven

My hands trembled slightly as I put my key in the lock. There was a gnawing in my stomach, and I only had myself to blame. I knew it was going to be bad, and the brief freedom I'd felt was dissipating. I psyched myself up, clenching my knuckles, holding my breath as I pushed the door open. He was going to make a big deal, he was going to shout and argue and insult me. He would call down my mother to look at what 'her daughter' had done.

He was going to call me ugly. And I was going to crumble.

And then I started to laugh. Because something so insignificant would take on these mythic 'good vs evil' proportions. Bloody ridiculous. So I slammed hte door with as much force as possible and waited for the show to begin. Let him be angry.

I looked in the mirror in the hallway. My hair was gone, hacked off, light and feathery. It had been long and dark, down to my waist, like a good Greek girl's should. And now it was all gone, poking out only as far as my earlobes. The girl who looked out at me was completely different, lighter. I tucked a small strand behind my ear, and smiled at my reflected self. It wasn't even awful. And I had expected it to be, almost wanted it to be.

Maybe I was overreacting, assuming my father would get annoyed about a haircut. He had bigger things to worry about, big horrible sad things to deal with.

'What the hell have you done to yourself?' His voice rang out from behind me.

Sadly, I had the benefit of experience when it came to my family's issues.

I turned to my Dad, unshaven, as was the mourning tradition. His bristles were growing grey, and his usually tanned face looked pale and drawn. He looked small and feeble, like an old man. Except that his cheeks were growing red, and his hands were waving around as he looked at me, unable to find the words. It would take him a second, but he'd find them. A lot of them.

'It's a haircut, Dad, a little perspective, please.'

I walked passed him to the kitchen, suddenly aware that after years and years of fights with my father, I had never worked out the right way to get around him. Talking logically didn't work, screaming back didn't work, getting upset didn't work. So generally belittling his point of view and acting like a petulant teenager until he gave up was the only option left.

'That is not a haircut! Nina!' He yelled up to my mother, 'Come down here and see what your daughter has done to herself.

'Elena, how could you be so irresponsible? What will people say when they look at you?'

'Erm, I assume they'll say "Hi Ellie, your hair is none of my business",' I smirked as I put the kettle on.

'Watch that mouth young lady, you're living under my roof-'

'And your rules limit me from changing my physical appearance in any way?' I felt that wave of nausea I always got when arguing with him, like there was something terribly wrong with me that I could never correct. 'That's certainly never been a problem before, Dad.'

'And what exactly does that mean?'

I rolled my eyes and exhaled. My mother entered the kitchen warily, she knew the alarm bells well. Round one thousand, it seemed. Ding ding ding. Ever since I'd moved back home after university the fights had become more and more difficult to avoid. More meaningless words shouted at each other. A new outfit, dying my hair, piercing my ears. And I *knew* it would piss him off. Part of me would probably have been disappointed if he didn't react. It occurred to me for the hundredth time that other people's families probably weren't like mine. Or maybe they were. Maybe there were families across the country arguing about how the word 'why' sounds insolent, or whose fault it is that the sprinkler isn't working. I really hoped not.

'When did you decide to do that?' My mother smiled, reached out her hand to ruffle my hair.

'A few minutes before I walked into the hairdressers.' Mum got it. She knew why I did things like that. She knew that desperate need to fix something, do something, anything to change who you are. Mum did it when she ran away from home, left Ireland for London, and never looked back. And the look she gave me as she stroked my cheek told me she knew that. She'd rather I shaved my head and got a new piercing every day than run away. It didn't change anything for her.

'Your head must feel a lot lighter,' she smiled, 'I like it.'

'What is wrong with you?' My father stamped his foot and lit a cigarette, flicking his lighter violently. He turned to my mother, 'Can't you just back me up for once? She's done something stupid, we're meant to punish her!'

'What stupid about a haircut, Nickos?' My mother implored, hands on hips.

'It's a rash decision-'

'It's a change.' My mother pointed out.

'And we've had enough change without Elena deciding she has to be the centre of attention again.'

He turned to look at me, 'You look ugly, you don't even look like you. You've ruined yourself.'

I took a deep, shaky breath and felt my eyes sting. 'I'll say it again, it's a haircut.'

'You do what you like, you always do. Put yourself before your family,' He stubbed the cigarette out into an ashtray and walked passed me. '*Putana*' he muttered, and a few seconds later I heard the TV blaring.

Mum looked at me in shock, her green eyes wide, her mouth in a small 'o'. She moved to go after him and I grabbed her arm, shaking my head. 'Don't get into another fight on my behalf.'

She just shook her head in disbelief, and ruffled my hair with a small, sad smile. 'It suits you.'

'Whore,' my father said.

Chapter Twelve

I'm sixteen, and it's a dreaded Sunday. We're sitting in Pizza hut, and I'm miserably picking at a side salad whilst the rest of my family eat pizza.

'Are you sure you don't want some darling?' Mama asks, 'I can cut a piece in half if you want?'

'Don't discourage her,' my father snaps. 'It's good you're doing this Elena,' he says around a mouthful of food, chewing loud sticky sounds, 'no-one will want you while you're fat.'

'Nickos.' My mother widens her eyes in warning, but says nothing further. I stare at my plate of soggy lettuce leaves and cross my arms across my stomach.

'No really,' my father continues, his voice booming, and I looked around the other tables to see if anyone is paying attention, 'you're smart, and you're pretty, but if you stay like this no-one can love you.'

He burps and continues, 'not that I mind, don't have any boys knocking at the door, that's fine by me.'

Nicky is silent next to me, staring into the distance, and I look down to see his fingers curling around the underside of his chair, which has been shuffled closer to mine. Clenching and unclenching, one pinky finger stretched out towards my chair. It makes me feel a little better.

'Elena?' My father requires an answer, 'You agree, don't you?'

I look up and his smile is so genuine, so caring that I almost feel bad for being offended.

'You're right dad, life is all about aesthetics.' I don't sound as sarcastic as I want to. The sad thing is, I'm used to it, this public discussion of 'Elena's problem.' To be fair, the fact that they don't mention 'Nicky's problem' in public is only because having an overweight daughter isn't as much of an embarrassment as a son with a drug habit.

He's always done it, Dad, told me to my face how I need to fix myself, where I'm lacking. He thinks it builds character. But that doesn't comfort me much when I stand in front of a mirror wanting to throw up, so sure that when we go to dinner, whether we have guests or not, my plate will be scrutinised, my fork movements counted. I always have to have a glass of water when I start to feel self-conscious. This desperate thirst, pure water to fix everything, settle the fears. And years later, the thirst will be from the dehydration out clubbing, the MDMA, the hangovers.

'I'm glad you understand, darling,' my father's voice drones on, pleased to be conversing on his favourite subject, 'I'm your father, I'm allowed to tell you the truth, aren't I?'

I'm allowed to insult you, is what he means, I'm allowed to say what I want without caring how you feel, because I'm your father.

'Of course you are, Dad.' I stare at my plate, and put a cheerful inflection into my voice.

Then of course, the waiter comes, or Nicky pretends to choke on his water, or Mum remarks on what we'll be doing tomorrow or next week, and we can all breathe again.

Dad loves the truth, loves being able to say exactly what he wants to people, straight to their faces. If you don't have the truth, you don't have anything, that's what he says. It's my fault that the truth he loves to tell me is always so painful. Or maybe it's my fault for not fixing myself. But I'll realise in the future that even if I could change to be what he wanted, the 'truths' would never stop.

The meal passes in a pleasant manner, once we've got that part out of the way, and by the time we leave, I almost forget he upset me. It's always easy to forget once it's done. Until the next meal.

But later that night I hear them arguing, Mum and Dad. Her berating him for being so rude, for not sugar-coating, for being too direct. It's an old argument.

'If I called you a fat bastard then, would that be okay?' I hear her voice clearly from outside the bedroom door.

'If it's true, then yes, although you don't need to be so aggressive about it.'

I hold my breath as I stand on the landing, keeping an eye on the floor, watching out for that one creaky floorboard.

'You can't say things like that to a sixteen-year-old girl, especially when you know she's so sensitive about the issue. It's cruel,' my mother reasons.

She's almost pleading, that tentative thread in her voice, begging for sanity, even though she knows he'll never change.

'Nina, for God's sake, she's fat. She needs to know that. No-one can love her the way she looks now.' I hear the springs sag as he slumps on the bed, 'I don't want her to go through life unloved. *That* would be cruel.'

My mother, exhausted, sighs and mumbles something like 'I don't believe you', before I hear the light click out.

I crawl into my bed, in the dark and cover my head with the duvet until it's too warm and stifling and hard to breathe. I wish, as I have more times than I wish to remember, that I have the guts to cut myself, make some real change. Better yet, cut off all the parts of me I can grab in my hands, too big and disgusting to be me.

Unloved. Unlovable. Surprisingly beautiful word. I hold my breath under the covers, until I'm ready to start crying, and I feel myself getting more hysterical, repeating the phrase 'no-one will love you' over and over in my mind until I start choking on the tears.

At some point in the early morning I stop listing the things I hate about myself, stop coughing and hiccuping and swallow the bile at the back of my throat. I open the duvet to allow a sudden burst of fresh air in, like a new beginning. Unlovable. Unlovable. No-one will choose me, and I will choose no-one, and it will be my choice. I won't love anyone, and there will be no chance to discover if Dad's right. I'll claim the phrase as my own. I will have no interest in boys, or sex or those Disney-movie endings that I used to love. Even the princesses fit a mold, and it doesn't match mine.

When I lay there in the dark, breathing heavy, emotionally exhausted, I promise myself he won't win. He never stops saying the things he says, his truths, and I never cry again.

Chapter Thirteen

Baby's always made me feel safe, and it wasn't just because Dex worked there. I'd been hiding out there for years, long before Dex and me became friends again, it was my safe haven. People don't usually go there unless someone shows you the way, a little cafe on a back alley of Leicester Square. Neon window lights, but dark leather booths, and the weirdest, most wonderful array of people.

Most nights, after I'd been clubbing and there was no pretty boy to cuddle, or a group of girls to whisper secrets with, I'd jump a bus to *Baby's*. Their signature is ice cream in the shape of other foods, vanilla and strawberry spaghetti, berry lasagne layered with vanilla and biscuits. Everything looks like something else. I loved it, because it was mine.

It was a good place to wait out the storm, anticipate the comedown. It had been a cherished little shelter for me whilst I waited for the tubes to start running at five am. And somehow, the comedown isn't as noticeable when you don't go to sleep, when you just let it slip away in between cups of black coffee. Waking up and finding the happiness gone feels like someone died.

And some days it was nothing to do with the drugs, or avoiding going home, it was just a place to be. Then Dex started working there, and I refused to give up my sanctuary for him. And whilst he didn't exactly apologise for all the stuff that happened when we were younger, he always brought me an extra scoop of ice cream. I'm very easily bought. So Dex became part of my life again. I owed *Baby's* for that. We never would have done that by ourselves.

So when I tried to tell Lee what was going on, sitting in her parent's house, in the kitchen we'd shared secrets in since we were kids, chowing down on chocolate fudge brownie that stuck in my throat, and realised I couldn't talk, couldn't tell her anything, I went to *Baby's*. It's nice to feel like something you have no physical hold on belongs to you.

Dex was in full management mode when I got there that afternoon, acting the host. Sometimes I was sure he only got that job because he's Italian, it lent an air of credibility to the place. He was the reason people ordered cappuccinos and biscotti, convinced that he'd come from a little town near Florence and started this fine establishment himself. Some afternoons I'd come by and find him talking with an accent. Dex was always a master at being what you wanted him to be.

'Bella bella!' He kissed me on both cheeks to complete the image, 'What's with the goth look?'

He gestured to my black dress, flared from the waist like a fifties house-dress. I wore it to the funeral. Funny how things you wear to funerals become attached to the moment. That will always be my 'funeral dress' now.

'You wear black,' I walked past him to my usual booth, and found myself relieved that it was empty. My maroon leather seating, matted with age. My table with the bent laminated menu with pictures of food. The little place strove for class, and then threw it away. It was trying hard, but was honest. I traced the tabletop, tacking from overuse, and smiled. Home.

No-one else was really around, a young family, a few teenagers, and a little old couple sharing a bowl of ice cream in such a sweet way that made my stomach hurt. It was the in-between time, after the afternoon Americans with their big hats and booming voices, and before the nighttime clubbers, desperate for the party to continue.

'I wear black expensive shirts,' Dex followed me, 'there's a difference. Maybe you should spend more money on your clothes.'

'I'm sorry, I didn't realise I was having a conversation with my father. Are you planning on serving me anytime soon?'

He raised an eyebrow at me, and I rolled my eyes. I flicked my nails and thought of a joint. A joint, and a hot bath, scalding hot so that the smoke and the steam intertwine, and I could turn off all the lights and just hear my own breathing.

Except I wasn't drinking, or smoking, or anything. And at home there was no talking, but always noises, someone checking the bathroom handle, smelling the scent from under the door, asking why why why I turned the lights out, wasn't that dangerous? Stupid? Why? And half the time, I didn't know why I did anything, except that it felt right.

'Yeah well, you dress like you're in mourning. People will think you're not having fun.'

'I'm not,' my mouth twitched, and I felt like a stroke victim, emotion fighting muscle.

'You go out more than anyone I know,' He tucked his pencil behind his ear, and his notepad in his back pocket.

'Doesn't mean I'm having a good time.'

'Then why go?'

'What else would I do? Stay at home and listen to my parents complain about the contestant of Big Brother Twelve or some bullshit?'

'Snob.'

'Media whore.'

He straightened abruptly, noticing customers hanging in the entry way, 'and with that charming interaction, I've got to get back to work.' He walked a few steps, and then turned back, 'Ice cream?'

I smiled at him, 'Mona knows.'

Dex was different at *Baby's*, and I loved to see him like that. He was calm, in control, capable, completely at ease with his responsibilities. He has a way with people, and it was the perfect outlet for that. He flirted with the middle-aged women, gave the kids extra scoops of ice-cream, chatted about the match with the men. It was like he knew you personally, that he cared about you. He was made for that job. Started there, went full time when everyone else went off to uni or apprenticeships, worked his way up. Changeable hours, flexibility, and enough money to get completely wasted every weekend. It was exactly what he wanted.

I looked across as he schmoozed the latest customers, and watched their faces, open, smiling, completely taken in by him. Dex looked over at me and winked. He'd make a good con-man with that smile. He used it to his best ability on Fridays and Saturdays, I supposed, and it definitely got him places. Into girls knickers, usually.

Mona brought over my bowl of ice cream and cup of coffee, and we chatted for a while. Mona had become a friend on those late evenings and early mornings. She was constantly working, desperately pushing herself, and I loved to watch her too. She has this coltish look like she's not quite sure about anything, like she's waiting to bolt. These big green eyes that just take in everything. She's too quiet to be a great waitress, but she seems like a good friend. But whenever we've talked, it's been about small unimportant things. There's a painful sense of loss when

74

you find someone who could be a best friend, if you spent enough time, knew them well enough, but know you never will. You've missed the window.

'Dex wanted me to give you these,' She pulled a packet of smarties out of her apron and threw them to me.

'He's good.' I smiled, and started bashing the bag up, crushing them to put them on my ice cream, just as we had when we were kids.

'We didn't have any, he went to the corner shop to get them earlier. He thought you'd be in.' Mona smiled, and I had the sneaking suspicion that she thought he was wonderful. And he is, Dex, wonderful, best friend, but never permanent. He needed the one night stands as much as I needed the one night friends.

Mona smiled shyly, as if she knew what I was thinking, and handed me a bunch of napkins, 'need a pen?'

'I've got one, thanks,' waving it in front of her, and she nodded before returning to work.

When I came in really late or really early, I liked to doodle on the napkins. If I was coming down I couldn't do anything but drink black coffee and give my hands something to do. It was weeks before Dex told me Mona had been collecting the doodles I left on the table. So now I drew them just for her.

I wasted a good hour or two just watching other people, sketching them, slowly eating my ice cream until it became melted into milkshake. It got darker outside, and I watched as the customers changed, the few families went home just as the children hit their grizzly sugar highs, and the teenagers left to find alcohol. The only people who came in after that were a few pre-theatre tourists, and people who worked in the area.

I hadn't really noticed the time passing until Dex crashed down in the booth next to me, resting his head back, eyes closed.

'What time is it?' I asked.

'About midnight,' he stifled a yawn.

'Seriously, wow, I hadn't realised.'

' Yeah, you're one of those customers who won't fuck off,' he nudged me, and opened one eye to gauge my reaction.

I just smiled, 'thank you for my smarties.'

'You can thank me with a shag later.'

I leaned my head on his shoulder, and just smiled. It felt normal, banter with Dex, it was the most normal I'd felt all week. We stayed like that for a few minutes, until I realised I'd never really shared silence with him. I was suddenly very aware of needing to say something, but he got there first.

'Why am I doing this?' He whispered, eyes still closed. 'Working here, not going to uni, still living with Dad?'

'You said you didn't want to move out,' I sat back to look at him, 'and this way you've got enough money to get drunk every weekend, go where you like, buy the nice shirts you like, anything you want.'

He took a deep breath and opened his eyes, sitting up, but staring at the table. He tousled his dark hair, and I realised he really didn't look so different from that ten year old boy who used to push me over in the playground, and put chewing gum in my hair. I tucked my now short hair behind my ears. It hadn't been much longer than this when I'd had to cut it after the chewing gum incident. Dad had been angry then, too.

'I like it,' Dex said suddenly, 'your hair, I mean.'

'You do?'

76

'It's different, you just keep changing on me. You're never scared to be different. Look at you, working in that art gallery, selling on the stalls, trying to make art. I should be doing something, something important.'

'If it helps, I'm not doing a very good job of it,' I shrugged, 'I don't feel like I'm doing a very good job of anything at the moment. I just feel like everyone's panicking about getting a job, losing a job, carrying on doing something they hate forever.'

'I'm scared of doing something I don't love forever.' He admitted, brown eyes surprisingly honest.

'Well, that's every Saturday night for you darling, isn't it?' I grinned, relieved to make it less of a Big Conversation. That wasn't me and Dex at all.

'Maybe I'm thinking of giving it up, the girls, the drinking, all of it.'

'You couldn't give up the drinking, you love it.'

He turned his body towards me, rolling up the sleeves of his black shirt that kept slipping down. Earnest little boy face, looking up from under those Bambi eyelashes of his.

'Well, let's do things the right way then, finally.'

'What right way?' I asked.

'Me and you. We start dating. After a while we get married, have very attractive children with symmetrical faces and hand them off to our parents so we can keep clubbing, pubbing and laughing every weekend. Sound good?'

I smiled, cynical and loved all at once, 'Sure darling, and when do you want to start this dazzling romance?'

Dex lifted his hands up above his head and stretched, feline, reaching up to the ceiling, and then relaxed. 'I don't know, in about four or five years? I think I'll have sorted myself out by then.'

'Me too, I hope.'

'So,' he wiggled his eyebrows, 'is this a plan then?'

I twitched my mouth, and imagined these dark haired symmetrical children, and clubbing into my forties and laughing every night. There was something nice about knowing everything there was to know about someone, knowing he could never hurt me, that we'd already been through our drama, and were best friends. A life without extremes could be quite nice. But then I thought about how I never wanted to get married, how Dex would never settle down, eventually he'd slip back into the sleeping around and knock up some girl, and feel obligated to take care of her. It was kind of surprising it hadn't happened already. There might be a little boy or girl out there who had Dex's hair or dark eyes, his cheeky smile.

'So you're saying when you get bored of sleeping around, in five years time, you want to get married and make babies with me?' I raised an eyebrow.

'Well, I meant it as a compliment.' He raised his hands up, and looked shocked when I stood up to go. I patted his hand to show I wasn't upset.

'I don't know if that's worse.' I walked to the front and handed Mona the money and my drawings. There were a few of the older couple sharing their ice cream. Seeing old people still in love made me feel...sad and happy and lost. Maybe it's just a continual and consistent lowering of expectations, until all you need to be happy is toad in the hole on Friday nights, and watching films together on Sunday afternoons.

'Sorry, it's not very good.' I told Mona, and she smiled at me, and shook her head.

'You always say that, and they're always wonderful. Hurry up and get famous, will you? I've got quite the collection of artwork.' She was so much younger than I realised, so that when she smiled, constantly tucking her hair behind her ears, she looked surprised by everything.

'I'll do my best,' I waved goodbye, and Dex walked me to the front door, where he took a minute to light a cigarette, perching outside like a true Italian cafe owner. Except that he was sitting under an umbrella, and it was starting to rain, the London lights of traffic and street signs bouncing off the damp pavement.

'I thought you quit?'

'Well, I'm quitting everything else, I've got to have one vice, haven't I?' He nudged me. Dex was gorgeous in his self-assurance, that complete understanding of who he was. He could be taller, or stronger, or more toned, but his smile was honest, and when he wanted to be serious, it was like his face didn't know how to accommodate. Every memory I have of Dex is of him smiling.

'Believe me, we've all got more than enough to go around,' I took a toke on his cigarette, comforted that I could, that I had someone that I could steal a cigarette from, who wanted to be my back-up.

'So, you haven't given me an answer,' his voice was delicate, and he looked out at the moving traffic. I suddenly thought of his mum, his beautiful mum who ran away, just disappeared one day, and never came back. He wanted to tie me to him. Little boy, I'm not going anywhere. But marriage doesn't tie anyone together, does it? And how to say any of that to the man standing in front of me without making him embarrassed and ashamed.

'I've got a few years to decide, right? So I'll check my crystal ball and let you know.'

He shrugged, a brief smile, and I threw my arms around him, knowing that I needed to be nicer.

'Love you,' I said.

'Love you too.'

I stepped out into the night, bright lights everywhere, walking to the bus stop amidst the noise. I pulled up my hood, wrapped my coat around me, and thought about Dex, about how much I had loved him when he was younger. How I'd always thought, somewhere along the line, that he would be it, eventually. That's what television teaches us, right? The best friend is never just the best friend. And finally, he looks at me, and sees me, and wants some sort of normal life together, and I want more. I want someone to make my pulse race, to make me thinking I'm drowning, whether that's good or bad. I judge Dex for sleeping around, and he judges me for the drugs, but I never get that itching in my stomach when I think of him with other women. He's just Dex.

When I sat on the bus, illuminated yellow flickering above me, I closed my eyes and thought about going home, about going back into that grey house, where no-one was talking. Where Dad walked out of the room when I walked into it, where Mum looked drawn and tired, and Nicky hadn't left his room for days. I looked down at my black trainers, the ones I'd painted daisies on, delicate petals and sparkling yellow centres. They were starting to run with the rain, and I watched as the white dripped onto the grey floor of the bus. By the time I got home, they were plain black again.

Chapter Fourteen

We're in Cyprus, under the veranda, a canopy of purple grapes keeping out the sunlight. My uncle keeps reaching up and picking them for us, throwing us one each, me, Nicky and Gali, but he can't snap the branches and pulls up the whole vine.

'Christos, sit down, you hurt yourself.'

'Yes Mama,' he mumbles, and drops into the chair, frowning. Me and Gali try not to laugh at her Daddy getting told off, and move closer to Yiayia as she reaches up above her head, and simply snaps the stem. She hands us a heavy bunch of grapes, dusted and engorged, with a flourish.

'Eat!' She commands, throwing her hands in the air, smiling. We chomp away happily for a quiet moment, and I watch her, my grandmother, thinking that she only ever smiles when we're here. When we're outside, in the gardens or by the sea. When I see her in Cyprus I can't imagine how she lives in that Big Old house, with grey stone, and clunky central heating. This is where she belongs.

'Everything useful, yes?' She tells us, rolling one of the leaves from the vine around her fingers. She passes it to us, and I reach out a finger to stroke it, warm and somehow furry. Gali does the same, and then shrugs. Nicky nods at Yiayia to continue.

'What...what do you mean?' Gali's voice is little, and she seems to shy to everyone but me. We're wearing matching clothing again, as we always tend to. Our mothers buy the clothes together, and think it's cute, but we don't complain. We're our own little army, solidarity marked by uniform of blue polka dot shorts, white t-shirts and matching blue hair bobbles.

'Earth, Mama Earth. You know her, yes?' Yiayia points to the stone beneath our feet, the leaf in her hands, the grapes, and then out to the sea in the distance, 'Everything we need, get from Mama Earth. Grapes for juicy, for water. Leaf for *koubebia*, for cooking. See? Be nice to Earth, it give everything. Everything useful.'

Gali looked at me to check if I understood. We didn't quite get it, but we knew we liked the grapes, and liked *koubebia*, the mincemeat rolled tightly in the dark green wraps that did look like those leaves Yiayia was holding. We liked swimming in the sea, and climbing on the rocks on the beach. We liked the earth.

'This is where we come from, this us.' Yiayia says, tapping the ground with her foot, 'Too young, dahlinks, you understand one day.'

She gives Nicky a significant look, like she knows he understands, he always understands. He sits with her, holding her hand and discussing in whispered Greek, as me and Gali see how far we can spit the grape seeds off the side of the veranda. 'Such a good boy, *lavendi-mou*' we hear, as always, and it's comforting. Nicky is beloved, but we could never blame her, he's first born, first boy, favourite. But we love him too. Other people tell me about their big brothers, how they tease them, hurt them, call them names. Nicky never does anything but smile and try to help me. Besides, I have Gali. We run off to play with the bunnies in their hutch, their little noses twitching, and I plan to ask Mama for one at home. A little bunny called *Koubebia,* me and Gali decide, because bunnies like leaves too.

And then of course, the family comes pouring out into the garden, aunties and uncles who kiss us and pinch our cheeks, call us little ladies or big girls. The older cousins call us 'cute' and drag us up to their rooms to dress us up like dollies, put their make-up on us. We sigh and go along, and return looking like clowns in plastic jewellery and rouged cheeks, scowling for the camera.

There's a long meal where the adults talk in Greek and the children don't talk at all. Gali understands, so she listens and translates if something is interesting. It usually isn't.

We eat with our fingers, grilled halloumi soft in the middle, with crisp salad that tastes of lemon. Then spiced meats and slippery rice that tastes like pasta, potatoes in a red clay pot. Dips and olives and pitta bread on the barbecue that cracks cracks when you pull it apart, burning your fingertips.

'Elena, *ella kori*, try this!' My father beckons me, a heavy hand on my head, holding out his glass, 'do you want to try?'

I shrug, embarrassed by everyone watching me. He regards me carefully.

'Eh, you won't like it anyway,' he laughs loudly and goes to take the glass back.

'Yes I will, you don't know!' I say instantly, irritated, and reach for it, taking a big gulp. My throat burns and my eyes water and I tell myself if I cough everyone will think I'm a stupid little girl. 'Lovely,' I say, and have another sip just to show them all. Everyone laughs, and I run back to my seat.

'Was it brandy?' Gali whispers.

'It was disgusting,' I reply.

'Yes, that's brandy.'

The night drags on and the crickets come out. Our cousins climb the trees to catch them in jars, and proceed to chase us round with them. The night air is warmer somehow, and I'm carried to the car by my father, half asleep against him, high up and steady and safe.

The leather seats are warm and sticky, but smell like every holiday I've ever been on. I rest my head on Nicky's shoulder, but wake up fully as my parents start to argue.

'We should have left earlier, they're tired.'

'We couldn't! It's my family!'

'Should you even be driving, the amount you had to drink?'

'It's safe, it's Cyprus!'

'It's dark, there are no road lights or signs and we're on the side of a fucking mountain!'

They carry on bickering, quietly at first then louder, talking over each other, shrill and angry.

'Nicky,' I ask sleepily, 'why didn't we get to say goodbye to the bunnies?'

He pauses, and clenches his fists as my parents continue.

'Because they were in the stew. We ate them for dinner.'

I throw up violently over the backseat of the land-rover, crying and flushed, with a knot in my stomach. Dad pulls over to the side of the road, and Mum cleans me up with a bottle of water that had been left in the car, body temperature and tasteless. She leaves the car door open to use the light, and wipes my wet eyes with a tissue. I reach out to her wet eyes and do the same. They're silent the rest of the way home.

Chapter Fifteen

I crashed into the house about ten pm, after another shitty day at the gallery. Another two teenagers who swore at me, another toilet that clogged. Paul didn't have time to look at my portfolio. Shocker. Dad was going to win. Law school. I'd sat at Baby's for two hours trying to work out a game plan. But I had no answers. I was an unemployed artist, and it was hardly a surprise.

The house was almost silent, and I felt it envelope me as soon as I walked in, tense and dark. Dad would be out, working, mourning, drowning his sorrows. I tried very hard not to ask myself what my Dad would be doing out at ten pm. I didn't let myself think about it, and in truth, I was relieved when he wasn't there to look at me and let me know what a disappointment I was. Nicky would be in his room, possibly reading or watching TV. I occasionally saw a flash of dark hair as he ran into or out of the bathroom as I was getting ready in the morning. But I hadn't talked to him since the funeral.

Mum would be reading in her bedroom with the TV on low in the background. There would be a plate left out on the side in the kitchen, covered in foil. She always left me whatever dinner had been served, and it was likely that she had eaten alone again. More and more it seemed that when I went home, there were three foil-covered plates lined up on the side, and my mother up in bed. Passive aggressive or simply thoughtful, I didn't know.

The air smelled smoky when I opened the door, and I wondered if Nicky had caved and been smoking in the house. I couldn't blame him. Except it had that sweet, woody edge to the scent, one that I recognised immediately. If Nicky was smoking weed, then that was a much bigger problem.

shouted, dumping my bag by the door, a sick
in my stomach.

re!' Mum called out, and I followed her voice to the
en. The smoky smell was stronger there, and the
t thing I noticed was the two plates of shepherd's pie
the side. My father's waiting plate had become a staple
ver the years, a symbol that he'd be out. Most days he'd
ome home and chuck out the food anyway, annoyed that
it had gone cold or soggy in the four or five hours since
Mum had made it. My waiting plate had become more of
a regular occurrence, and it made me feel guilty.

'Mum, are you smoking?' I half-smiled, and as I looked up
she brought her hands from behind her back to reveal a
rollie. The back door was wide open, and the darkness
outside only served to white wash her. She looked little,
this small woman with the oversized jumper and the
leggings with the holes in. Her hair was free and frizzy,
but looked distinctly auburn. When I was a kid I used to
think Mum's hair was more red when she was angry, but
now I'm sure it's her life force that's drained away. Little
old woman, with a dippy smile and her eyelids stooped
low.

'Guilty! Sort of!' She waved the cigarette around, and I
suddenly realised it wasn't Nicky.

'Mama, is that what I think it is?'

'If you think it's a marijuana cigarette, then yes, your
assumptions are correct! Ding ding! Ten points to Ellie!'

'Oh sweet Jesus,' I sighed, 'I'm putting the kettle on.'

My mother giggled, 'Oh, how very British of you darling,
yes, put the kettle on. Tea is very important.'

'Would you like a cup of tea?' I talked slowly and clearly,
although I didn't know why. I'd been stoned, most people
I knew had been stoned at one point or another, and they

understood things perfectly fine. They usually craved tea. But it was my mother, and though Nina had surely been a wild child, she was a grown up now. Maybe other people's parents were cool like that, but in my mind she was conservative, she was a mother, first and always.

'No thank you! I've got wine.' She pointed to the empty glass on the kitchen table. 'Oops, guess I don't!' She went to refill it as I clicked on the kettle, the loud noise covering up any questions I wanted to ask. It gave me breathing time, as I waited for the hot water, steeped the tea bag, added the milk. Squeezed and drained, and swirled. Three stirs to the right and one to the left.

'You know,' my mother said, staring in surprise at the remains of the paper burning her fingertips, 'I haven't rolled a cigarette in twenty-five years. Can you believe that? I did a pretty good job, I think.'

'Yes, I'm very proud,' I said, blowing on my tea to cool it, and sitting down at the table. I gestured for her to sit with me.

'Oh, we're stepping into your office, are we Doctor?' She smiled wryly, but flicked the butt out into the garden, and pulled the backdoor closed, shivering briefly and rubbing her arms. She was barefoot, and I knew she would have been padding about on the grass in the dark, despite it being cold. It had rained that day, and she loved to walk on wet grass, to smell it. She said it felt like being home.

'So, what's going on?'

She smiled grimly, stared at the table top, took a sip of her wine, and I saw how her mouth was plum stained and smeared. Her lips were chapped and her skin was lifeless.

'It's not much really. Just, in the light of all this death I've realised I have been unhappy for a very long time.

Most of my life in fact. And what's the point of being unhappy 'til you die?'

I opened my mouth to reply, but really had nothing to say. She was unhappy? She'd always been unhappy? Just like Yiayia, never really smiling, never really feeling anything. Except, my mother used to smile all the time, used to laugh all the time...

'Oh, I don't mean you, love! Or Nicky. You have brought me the most joy, you've stopped my life from being worthless. But I'm not really ready to just live through you yet, you know? Be a grandmother and stuff.'

'Well, thank goodness for that,' I said, thinking of Dex's idea. Mum would love that.

'It's just, life is so fucking long,' she reached out to stroke my hair, her vowels softening over the swearing, 'but it's too short to be unhappy. And I'm unhappy.'

Part of me felt like shouting 'Why is everyone so fucking unhappy?' and I started to think I didn't know anyone who was truly content, or if they were it was a lie, an eyes-closed wish because we were stupid little humans who live and worry and die, and that's it.

Life seemed ridiculous, just then, as I sat with my stoned mother and sipped my tea. Life seemed to be this thing that involved mortgages and taxes and babies and planning for a moment, somewhere, when you got to breathe. And all I could think was that my mother was the best person I knew, that she was kind, and gentle and beautiful and smart. And she wasn't happy. So what chance did I have? The only thing I had that she didn't was youth, twenty grands worth of debt to The Student Loans Company, and a casual drug habit. And even that was questionable.

'So, whatcha gonna do about it?' I asked her, aware that we'd both been quiet for a really long time.

'Travel, I guess? See things, do things, while I still can?' She was like a child, asking for permission, and she must have realised it because she grinned, 'After that I'll come back and settle for being a grandma and knitting and be completely satisfied, I promise!'

'Sounds like a good idea, Mama.' I patted her hand, 'I don't want you to be unhappy.'

'I don't think I will be for long. It's just one of those nights, you know?' She sighed, tracing the rim of her wineglass.

'Those nights seem to be happening more and more.' I got another wine glass from the cupboard and we finished the bottle between us. Then I reached into the teapot on the shelf above the sink, and retrieved a squashed packet of cigarettes, offering them to her.

'You knew?' She smiled, looking guilty.

'You moved them from behind the vodka in the cabinet last week,' I teased, 'should have known I'd look there.'

We sat quietly, and she smoked a cigarette with the back door open again, and I threw the remainder of my tea away to concentrate on my wine.

'So, where did you get the weed, anyway?' I asked gently, worried about Nicky, what it could mean.

'From your room. I can guess your hiding places too, it seems.'

At that point, I didn't even care that she'd been snooping in my room, or taken my drugs without asking, I was relieved.

We finished our drinks, talking about all the places we wanted to see, to experience, and sometimes, I realised, I was more like my mother than anyone else. It was comforting to have someone who had the same dreams as you, wanted the same places, the same adventures. Except that she'd missed her chance for them so many times. We laughed, though. We talked, and laughed, and when the angry little clock on the wall crowed midnight, we washed up our wineglasses and dried them, and carefully placed them at the back of the cupboard, as if to hide the evidence. Midnight, when we trudged up the stairs, my hand on her arm to steady her. Midnight.

I didn't ask where Dad was.

Chapter Sixteen

We're sitting in the living room, waiting for the hearse to arrive. My dress is too small, and my tights are woollen and itchy. I trace a nail down my leg, trying to be subtle.

'Elena! Behave yourself!' My father commands, and I turn to look at him with a frown. Yiayia walks past and places a hand on my head. She looks comfortable in her black dress and her heavy gold cross. She seems strong and large and able to deal with this, whilst the rest of us rush about, confused.

'*Thelis chai*, dahlink?' She says, stroking my hair roughly.

I say no, but there's a various chorus of replies.

'I'll make it Mum, you sit down.' *Theo* Christos says, and starts towards the kitchen, before her voice cuts through.

'Christos! I look invalid? No? *I* make tea!' She grumbles a bit in Greek, the phrase I recognise as 'Mother Mary, give me strength!' and starts towards the kitchen, slow but determined. She's left her pillbox on the table next to my chair. It's pretty, an octagon of silver, with little blue beads encrusted around the edge. When I open it, it has a purple velvet lining, and multiple white pills leaving a chalky residue on the purple. I wonder why Yiayia has a special box for her mints, and put it back down before anyone shouts at me.

Gali comes to sit on the edge of the armchair, her hair tied back like mine, her black dress exactly the same as mine. But her shoes have pretty silver buckles, and she's been allowed to wear earrings. Any other time we'd all have been here, eating soup, trying to find hiding places for all the fruit we'd been given, making jokes about domestic science class and finding a Greek husband. As I think this, I look down and realise this is his chair, I shouldn't be sitting in his chair. Gali seems to realise this at the same time as me, and we back away.

We decide to stand by the front door for a while, looking for the hearse although we don't really know what it is, and we don't want to ask.

'Is Nicky coming?' she whispers.

'I don't know.'

'You haven't heard from him?'

'A few phone calls. He's in Manchester. He said he was safe.'

I want to cry already, but it's not for Pappou, it's for Nicky. I miss Nicky, Nicky who ran away weeks ago, and told me he was coming back, that he'd never leave me, not really.

'The car's here,' my uncle announces, and we all file out to look at the casket in this car with the boot open. We make stupid comments about how nice the flowers are, even though we're the only ones who brought them. Bright yellow daffodils in the grey morning, against the black of the cars and our clothes.

A bald man holding a top hat and cane asks for the grandchildren. Me and Gali walk forward, because Nicky's not there.

'Kids, would you like to say goodbye to Pappou?' He gestures towards some incense sitting in front of the coffin, and we don't know what he wants us to do. The adults won't explain it, so we just say 'no thank you' and back away, until our ankles hit the curb. We watch from there as our parents move the smoke around in the air, making symbols, saying prayers.

And then our parents are making 'chkk chkk' sounds and we're bundled into black limousines, our dresses squeaking on the leather seats as we slide across.

'When's Nicky coming back?' Gali's voice is small, 'I miss him.'

'Me too,' I whisper, the tears starting already, 'I don't think he's coming back.'

The rest of the ride is silent, stuck in traffic. It's not like all the glamourous people on TV, riding in these big fancy cars. It's just sad and quiet, and I don't think we're allowed to speak.

When we get to the graveside after the church, there's a figure in an oversized black suit, so large that it seems to be hanging off of him. A skeletal thin stranger who looks nothing like my brother, with these huge eyes that seem too big for his face. He drags his thumb and forefinger across his chest tapping irregular patterns, agitated. He scratches at his arm, picking trough the jacket sleeve like it's killing him. He won't look at me, just concentrates completely on the priest, copying his movements, and I copy Nicky's. His skin is like gauze, and I remember my brother was always tanned, no matter what time of year it is. He's tried to shave, but it hasn't worked, there's little cuts all over his face.

My mother cries before the ceremony finishes, and my father drags me away by the hand, mumbling to himself about the embarrassment. I want to go to Nicky, and I see him with Yiayia, talking. She strokes his hair, and hands him an envelope. They stand by the table set by the graveside, the food to honour the dead. I see him take a piece of bread, forcing himself to chew. He swallows the *commaderia* easily, which I hate, but I drink some anyway, because that's what you do. Dad won't let go of my arm, because he knows I want to go to Nicky, thinks I'll cause

93

a scene. It's like he's protecting me. He's lost one child, he won't lose another. He thinks Nicky will steal me away. Eventually, Dad gets distracted, and I push my way through the black suits and high heels to where I saw my brother last. He's gone. Gali shrugs, and Yiayia strokes my hair gently.

'Is okay,' she says, 'Be alright.'

I won't see my brother again for three months.

Chapter Seventeen

'I really didn't think you'd show,' Daniel admitted as I swung my legs back and forth, sitting in the chair in his studio. It was a week day, and somehow it felt important that it wasn't just me stopping by on a Sunday, in between work. I'd come to see him.

'Why?' I looked around the sterile little room, practically a cupboard inside that big building. Black and white photos of his work were framed on the walls, some simple and small, some big celtic knots that covered entire backs, complex and delicate, shaded. His portfolio. He was an artist. And his art lived forever, it breathed and moved and defined people. I was almost jealous.

He looked up at me and raised an eyebrow, 'because I thought after last time I'd pretty much pissed you off so much you wouldn't come back.'

'Were you trying to do that?'

'Nah, it's natural talent,' he smirked, fiddling with his glasses. I liked looking at him, finding the lines of him, framing him as if I was sketching a portrait. He was all angles, the dark hair naturally messy, circular and soft compared to the rest of him. He just didn't look like a tattoo artist. The others in Eclipse, the skinny punk boys in black and the girls in rockabilly dresses with half-sleeves inked in bright colours, they fit. Daniel looked like anyone else. I assumed he had tattoos, he couldn't possibly make all that art for other people and never once explore his own canvas. But all those others were walking adverts for their own work. He wasn't, whatever he had, it was hidden away.

'So, am I stopping you from working, or something?'

'No, I'm pretty much the substitute,' he sighed a little, picking up things from around the little room, bottles of ink, photos, pictures, rearranged the design folders stacked up on the side. 'I get the walk-ins, you know? The teenage girls who want flowers and butterflies. I ink the girls who will probably regret it in ten years time. I intimidate them less, you know?'

He was being punished for being nice.

'Plus they probably don't want to be inked by someone who's making it clear how stupid they think their design is. Like it's below them.'

'Yep, so I'm the nice guy. Except it means I never get the good stuff, the big projects.' He gestured at the walls, a sad little look on his face. 'Anyway, what about you?'

'Me? I haven't been making much art recently.'

'No?'

'No.'

'Why?' He seemed to always be leaning on something, never standing upright. Always an S-shape against a surface.

'Because I don't feel like it.' I snapped, and instantly regretted it. He shrugged and looked down at the ground. I bit my lip and counted the cracks in the ceiling. I got to fourteen before I apologised.

'Sorry, I'm just...not used to...this.'

'Talking?'

'Getting to know people.' I stopped, 'Sober, I mean.'

He nodded, twitched his mouth up and I figured we were okay.

'My cousin's getting married,' I blurted out suddenly. He tilted his head to the side, amused.

'Oh really?'

'She can't tell anyone, because of my grandmother's...you know. You're not allowed to have good news at a time like this...It's disrespectful.'

'You think it would help. People want good news, don't they? Desperate to cheer themselves up, I'd have thought.'

'Happiness is a choice, and you've got to reign it in to respect the dead. And Gali, she's good like that, she won't tell anyone, won't celebrate. We're not meant to drink anyway, or take drugs or anything else. Bad stuff, you know?'

The words wouldn't stop pouring out and I felt like it was Daniel's fault, that he was good at listening, that he could stop me at any point if he just knew me a bit better, if he knew anything about me, if he was my friend, I wouldn't tell him. But he was a stranger, and strangers never tell you to shut up.

'We're meant to mourn for forty days, be completely...pure. And she's so happy, Gali, you know? But she's not allowed to show it. And she never wanted to get married, never! But it's like she can't believe how lucky she is. And they're all going to ruin it, judge it as soon as they find out.'

'Who's they?'

'The family. Big family. Big judgemental family.' I sighed, and flicked my nails, my stomach dropping at the thought of what they would say behind her back, what my father would say, how they would ruin it.

'Big family can be nice.' And I knew then that it was just him, which I should have guessed, in that little flat in Clapham. Alone in a dingy flat, alone at work where he didn't fit.

97

'Sometimes friends are more important.' I shrugged, and he smiled again. I remembered some of his friends from that night, students, a bit younger than him, more excitable, more eager to do this, and that, and everything, all at once. He was the one keeping tabs on all of them, looking after them, advising. He stopped them from taking everything at once, from going to the cash machine for a third time, when to stop on the drinks, when to head home. They were easy enough to handle, a group of scruffy enthusiasts, but he got it, whatever it was. That ecstasy was meant to open you up, make you a conduit to everything else. Make you open, inviting, loving. And completely free.

'Your mates, from the club, were they alright? There was that one guy who looked a bit screwed up.'

'Jimmy, yeah, he just never knows when to say no,' the smile was broader now, and I felt awkward as he looked me straight in the eye when he talked. I wasn't used to eye contact with people I didn't know almost as well as myself, 'He's a little young, a little desperate for everything to be right now. He'll learn.'

'You usually look after them all.'

He nodded, 'I don't normally spend the whole night talking to a girl and take her back to my flat, if that's what you mean.'

'It wasn't,' I insisted, 'I just meant...I don't know. Conversation is difficult.'

'Is it?'

'I don't know you,' I said.

'Then surely we have more things to talk about,' he wriggled his eyebrows, a move that made me instantly think of Dex, 'we could talk about the reason you're here.'

'Here?'

'In my...studio...'

'I-I...thought-'

'You want a tattoo, don't you?' He asked, knowing smile in place, and I breathed a sigh of relief.

'Well, actually, yes.' I jutted my chin out.

'You have a design on a piece of paper in your pocket, don't you?' he walked over and leaned against the chair next to me, 'go on, cough up, what's the plan?'

I felt nervous with him being so close, like my air wasn't my own.

'Okay,' I reached into my bag, 'around my ankle, but a different font, this.'

I handed over the scrap of paper and watched as he started to frown, and closed his eyes, taking off his glasses and pinching the bridge of his nose. He was disappointed.

'No,' he said.

'No? Just no?' I replied, working myself up for a fight, 'I thought you're not allowed to question customers choices?'

'You're not a customer. And I'm not letting you do this.'

'*Letting* me?'

He handed me the scrap of paper back. I looked down at my own handwriting. It simply said *Everybody Leaves.*

'What's wrong with it? It's what I think, how I feel.' I clenched my fists, glad to be back on terms where I could shout, scream and argue as much as I wanted.

'Yeah, it's how you feel *now*.' He sounded irritated, a vein in his neck suddenly apparent as his voice rose, 'You're in pain, and that's the only way to show it. But what happens when one day, someone doesn't leave? You'll push them away, because otherwise, you're a hypocrite!'

'You know nothing about me,' I said, deadly still. This was the end, it wasn't going to work, there had been no chance. My life was nice and quiet the way it was, I didn't need this.

'But I know everything about how you feel,' Daniel said quietly, and looking straight at me, pulled up the sleeve of his t-shirt until I saw tiny dark words etched on the underside of his bicep in spiky font: *The world has let me down.*

'Oh,' I said quietly, not looking at his eyes, focused on those angry little words. How hadn't I seen that the other night? Or perhaps I had, and had forgotten. I was so busy talking, marvelling at finding someone who understood me, man, yeah, completely, that I didn't look at how broken he was too. Used to be broken. Fixed up with superglue and gaffer tape. A fixer-upper. Second-hand model.

'Yeah,' he sighed, and letting go of his sleeve, let his hand rest near mine, almost touching.

'Did it? Let you down, I mean?' I whispered, and his head rested nearer to mine to hear me. I reached across to him, lifted the sleeve and traced those words, addicted suddenly to this version of my stranger. Daniel, cheerful, irritating Daniel, completely in control. He was angry, once. My fingertips followed the font as he whispered back.

'It did, or I did, people did. It happens, but it made me who I am, got me here.' His hand reached my neck and rested there, not pulling or pushing, just beautifully cold, calming. I felt my own pulse through the coolness.

'Are you happy?' I barely breathed the question, and watched him nod, seriously.

When he was silent, he was different again, his skin pale, his eyes light, and his hair as dark as the angry words etched into his skin. Visible scars. He was right, I wanted everyone to see how hurt I was, I wanted to never explain it, never talk about it, just have people look at me, and know I was broken, know I had a story and a secret, and they'd never know the extent. Depression is special, unhappiness is defining. Because it's easy to be happy, isn't it? Easy to see the beauty in things, with a half gram of MD and a bottle of champagne. A bar of chocolate, a joint on a Sunday evening. But what about without all that?

His cold fingertips traced my neck, and I felt myself shiver.

Chapter Eighteen

I'm thirteen the first time I smoke a joint. I don't get high, but I pretend. We're at one of Lee's infamous house parties, and she grabs me by the hand, physically drags me over to the cloud of smoke in the corner, where the cool kids sit.

They're all beautiful, all have these problems I can't even imagine. Which is why Lee's parties always end with someone climbing up the drainpipe or out of the bathroom window. Someone's anti-depressants mixing with the alcohol and making them set fire to their jacket in the garden. Someone jumping straight out of the closet onto the sofa with the nearest same-sex warm body. One girl lines up every beer bottle she finds on the garden wall and smashes them with a moulding tennis racket. I will never understand these people. And that's how I know they're special. Being suicidal is cool. Being depressed is cool. Drinking straight whisky and smoking roll-ups is cool.

We sit in a circle, and a boy I've seen at every one of these gatherings and have never talked to hands me the joint. I breathe in shallowly and hold it in my lungs, because I refuse to splutter and cough in front of these people. I am not a stupid little girl because I don't have any trauma. I've never cut myself, never doubted my sexuality. Never wanted to do drugs. And somehow that makes me feel boring, average.

It tastes like any other cigarette except for a sweet green aftertaste that turns stale on your tongue. I breathe out. I am so very, very cool.

The beautiful girls with the huge eyes and tiny waists ask me who I am.

I say that I'm friends with Lee and I want to be an artist. That's all I ever say when people ask me who I am.

'No, sweet thing, they want to know who you are. Really. Who.' This from a girl in the corner, slumped sideways in the armchair, staring at the ceiling. She looks like she has no structure, bends and falls wherever gravity forces her. The lights are off, but the backdoor is open with the porch light filtering though. Everybody looks a lot prettier than they are usually, and than they will by the end of the night.

I don't know what to say, and the joint's come back around. It's times like this I miss Dex fiercely. He'd be here to protect me, to show them my good side. He'd be one of those beautiful people, say the right thing, make them laugh, be accepted instantly. I never feel ugly with Dex, even after all the things he said to me, even after that awful fight. He'd look good smoking a joint, drinking neat whisky. He'd fit in here.

'They want your pain, darling,' an older girl with dirty blond hair says. Her eyes are rimmed with so much kohl, like an angry child's interpretation of a panda. I think it makes her look mysterious. She's drinking red wine from a tea-cup and the beautiful brown-haired boy at her feet reaches up, tangling his hand in her hair without a word.

'You've got to have a story. Tell us.' The girls my own age cling to the wiser one's words. They don't eat much at all, their bodies shrivelling in a way that at thirteen is coltish and attractive, but by sixteen will make them aged and skeletal. They are not unkind, but they think I'm a fraud. One of those friends who is good to have around on a fat day, to follow you round and tell you you're beautiful. To make you feel better about yourself.

I wrap my arms around myself, and Lee blows smoke in my face, giggling. Lee is their sage, their wise listener.

She's seen them at their worst, and hasn't judged them, and so she is holy. She doesn't need to be one of them, because they love her for who she is. Their messiah, their mentor, their confessor. ParentSisterFriend who makes them feel whole. Therapist, putting down the needles, bringing out the antiseptic.

What can I tell them, to prove I'm for real. Prove I've experienced pain. About Nicky, in love with something that never loved him back? How Mum still keeps methadone hidden in a brown cough syrup bottle in the back of the bathroom cabinet, and we know never to touch it? About the day my father told me I was a dreamer, a disappointment, and snapped my easel in half? The weight, the feelings of being useless, worthless, ugly? No, because these are normal, and they're mine. The times when Yiayia stares into space angrily, then suddenly focuses into real life, looks at me like I'm a stranger? These are mine, and they're so small and subtle and painful that no-one would understand. They can't have them, they're mine. So I lie.

I tell them a painfully elaborate story about my mother. That she was a Catholic, that she's from Ireland. That she wanted to abort me. That she is stuck in a loveless painful marriage, because religion wouldn't let her get rid of me. That I'm responsible for trapping her in a life she never wanted. They nod, and sigh, and stub out the joint in the ashtray.

'That's deep.'

'Mental shit to deal with, man, harsh, you know. So harsh.' The brown-haired boy looks at me with sympathy, and reaches out a hand to stroke my hair. He pulls back his hands from my ear like a magician, producing a little white pill with a star on it.

'Do you like sweeties, little girl?' He laughs, and then leans forward, so we're cross-legged together, shared space in the corner. 'No, really, it'll help. All that stuff fades away, and you realise you were happy all along. Happiness is just chemical.'

I shake my head shyly, because I think he's too beautiful to talk to me. I say no because that's what you're meant to do when someone offers you something, because I'm a good girl, and good girls say no. But I want to say yes to everything.

He squeezes my hand, that brown-haired boy, and washes the star down his throat with whisky from a wineglass. He shuffles back to the girl in the armchair, his head resting against her, and I feel weak and boring and like nothing ever changes.

Lee shuffles closer to me, 'I didn't know that about you, poor baby.' She rests my head against hers and I know she loves me more for the lie. I've become one of her flock, finally depending on her in that way all of the others do. She knows me now. I'm now perfectly loveable in her eyes, beautifully broken. At some point, too much time passes to ever take it back.

Over the years she will watch me warily when we discuss abortion in our religion classes, or when we discuss unwanted pregnancies in those 'what if' scenarios. Always keeping an eye on me, looking out for me.

I'll write it as a story and send it out into the world. I call it Unwanted, and I win a prize and some book tokens. My story was my lie, my own unwanted baby. I feel guilty for ever saying anything, feel pathetic for having no defining pain. I want to be depressed because depression is beautiful and happiness is chemical, and that's why people do what they do.

I don't smoke with the cool kids as they skin up again, but they nod with respect as I leave the circle, convinced that I'm for real. I don't feel high at all, but I pretend, use it as an excuse to sit under the kitchen table with Lee, eating gingerbread men. I bite off each limb first before finally devouring the head, and the thin, depressed girls watch in admiration.

Chapter Nineteen

I didn't mean to look. It was a complete accident, and I'll regret it forever. Not only for knowing, but for not doing anything. For the visual image I got, for the bile that rose to the back of my throat. For the way I faced him later that day, and managed to smile, managed to pretend, so, so easily. It's disgustingly easy to convince yourself nothing is wrong, to convince others that you're okay.

I'd picked up my Dad's phone, trying to get a phone number for the take-away that evening. As I did, a message came in, and automatically opened:

I've been thinking about you. I'm tied to a chair, waiting for you to fuck me. Where are you?

I wrote down the number on my wrist, put the phone back and hid upstairs for the rest of the night. Pretended I was too ill to eat dinner. Pretend, pretend. Spent the night trying to convince myself it was a practical joke from a mate, all a joke. Some meaning I'd missed, misinterpreted. I always loved to think the worst of people, that was all. I needed to give it a chance. But all I could think of was the flimsy excuses, the fact he was never home. That night I heard them arguing again, because Mum hadn't forced me to come down and eat dinner with them. Because she let us kids get away with everything.

After a night with no sleep, I decided I'd confront him. I got on the bus the next day, trundling along, slow as ever, for an hour, rehearsing over and over in my head what I'd tell him, how I'd do it. Would I embarrass him in front of his employees? Would I be still, silent, foreboding? Would he cry, would he apologise? Would he leave us?

But when I got there, he was in full 'selling' mode. Smiling, so pleased to see me, showing me off to his clients, going on and on about how proud he was of me, as if he knew what I was there to do, and he'd do anything to silence me. I knew it was all for show, but it still hurt.

He didn't once stop to look at me, constantly moving, talking loudly, introducing me to people I didn't need to meet.

'I'm very busy *kori,* sorry, can we talk at home?' He looked past me as he said it, and all I could see was images of him and this woman, this faceless bint strapped to a chair, and somehow texting at the same time.

I would blackmail him, I'd split up our family, and then where would he be? I'd tell him the truth about Yiayia, about how she died, how she didn't want to be with us anymore. That, most of all, would kill him.

But I couldn't. I nodded, and smiled and started to walk away.

'Elena,' he said, 'I know you're angry about the arguing. I'm bringing home flowers for your mother tonight.'

And he gave me fifty quid. So I caught the bus and then the tube, and wound up in Camden Market. Home. I went into the nearest pub, The World's End. Appropriate, because nothing ended, nothing changed. Not unless you were brave. And I wasn't.

Because he was my Daddy. And you don't tell your Daddy what to do, he's supposed to tell you, help you, guide you. I could believe it was a mistake, a joke, that I'd imagined it all. After four double vodka Redbulls I was not so optimistic. I couldn't stop shaking.

And after that, I still had all that cash he gave me. Why did he give me that much? Why give me money at all? So I was meant to spend it. So I found a dealer in the market who had some dodgy legal highs, and laughed with a dickhead who was also on something. We sat under the bridge, shared a joint and he talked about something he thought was important, whilst I wondered if my father was fucking his mistress now.

It got darker, and the pills started to make me buzz, and the joint made me feel sick. The druggie smiled, and pushed me back against the cold wall of the bridge.

'You're a fuckwit,' I told him, as he nodded, off his head to a tune I couldn't hear, 'You're a bully, and you're about to lose everything.'

He stared at me, brown unfocused eyes as his hand slide against my thigh through my jeans. My chest compressed and the words unfurled from me.

'I hate you,' I told him, 'I've always hated you.'

The druggie shrugged, and wandered off.

I could have gone to Daniel, so close, so close and willing to talk and listen and be there. But I didn't know him yet, and I didn't want anyone to know about my family. I get to judge, no-one else does. He was not my therapist. He wasn't my anything. And if I saw him I'd treat him horribly, I'd punish him. Trick him into thinking I wanted him, and then attack him for touching me.

I didn't want MDMA, I didn't want happiness. I wanted anger. I was a coward and I needed to suffer. After half a gram of coke, shaking out of my skin, I felt honest anger, when everything was numb and far away, and everyone seemed to be miserable anyway. Nothing really mattered. Everybody lies.

I chatted shit to strangers on the bus, crashed through the front door at two am, buzzing on something other than worry and regret until the next day began. And somehow, that was a relief.

Chapter Twenty

It's a bad trip. I've heard about them, K holes, acid flashbacks. Coke instead of MD, speed mixers, everything. You take a chance. You ignore all those ridiculous stories in the magazines of your youth about the girl who drank so much water she died, or had a reaction when she tried one pill. The boy who thought he could fly, but didn't try taking off from the ground first. They're not us, we don't care about them. They're stupid, we're smart. They're reckless, we're connoisseurs. They are the drunken fights and pints of stella to our excellent vintage of wine, followed by a night of mind-blowing intellectualism. Just because you buy your drugs from a boy named Stevo, who still lives with his mum at thirty-four and looks about sixty, does not mean the experience itself is sullied.

Except this time, I'm freaking out and I'm going to fucking kill Stevo, that pathetic arse.

I'm in a club, and everything is woozy and out of focus, flashing lights and dark faces, where everyone seems to stare and all the eyes are whiter than they should be. I hold it together, say nothing, but Lee notices how I can't stop staring at everyone. She seems to be saying words, but everything seems slow and deep. Her hands are making signals, but it's like I suddenly need glasses. My heart pounds, and I hear myself whine a little. Oh god, I'm going to be one of those girls I read about in J-17. I'm going to be a terrible warning to some little girl who was never going to try drugs anyway. And maybe I'll die, and they'll tell my parents why, and Nicky's shame will resurface. Maybe they'll blame him. Maybe they should.

I'm too hot, and I can't stand still, I have to move but everything is slipping through my fingers like rain, until

Lee grabs me, her hands invisible, but strong and clammy. I keep thinking her fingers are slipping from mine with the sweat, but they don't. She elbows and shoves, and I stumble after her until the cold night air hits me. I breathe deep.

'What's she taken?' I hear voices, far away. I look at my feet and watch as they sway.

'I don't know. Did someone spike her drink?'

'It's Ellie, she took something,' this is Dex, I'm sure of it.

'Oiieugh.' I try to say 'hey' but that noise was not what I meant.

'Shh, now darling, drink this,' Lee, I think, is stroking my hair, and a bottle of water appears, but I don't want it to hit my stomach. This isn't ecstasy. On ecstasy I wait for the chance to drink, revel in the water, the freshness and how it hits my stomach with a beautiful drop. Now all I want is my bed, the dark, and no-one looking at me like this is my fault. Oh god, getting home. Oh god.

'Ellie, sweetie, can I have your cloakroom ticket so I can get your bag?'

I reach into my back pocket and offer her everything I retrieve. She picks through receipts and change, and leaves.

'You really are a fucking moron, you know,' Dex's voice sounds really far away and unconcerned.

And you're a slag. 'Brrrurr skllllaaa.'

'Why do you have to do this? What made you so fucked up that you have to do this all the time? Why can't you just have a drink and a laugh like the rest of us?' I tilt my head slightly, and see his trainers. It's definitely him talking, 'I'm so tired of having to look after you.'

You don't look after me, you've never looked after me. All you've done is fuck around and use me when you need me and never listen to me, and use me as your personal agony aunt. You're not my friend. You don't know me at all. You're just here because I'm one of the two people in the world who won't sleep with you. Again.

'We're back! Got your bag! Do you want your hoodie?' Lee sounds too cheerful, and at the back of my mind, I think she's telling Dex to shut up in that wordless way she has.

'Caarf'

'Scarf, right.' Lee has years of experience dealing with drunken, misery-ridden people, and I get briefly upset thinking that I've become one of them, that I depend on her.

'Uff ooh.'

'I love you too, Ellie. It's all going to be fine, honestly.'

We start walking, and it's awful to see how the pavement bumps and shakes under my feet, but it's even worse when I close my eyes and feel my stomach clench around itself, so I keep my eyes wide and try not to focus on anything but breathing in the cool air.

We walk for what feels like miles, until eventually I click my jaw and find my tongue moves how I want it to.

'I'm...really sorry.'

'We know. It's okay.' Lee squeezes my hand and hands me the water bottle. It tastes divine.

'It's not,' Dex says, and strides off ahead.

'Ignore him, he's just annoyed because he was doing well with yet another conquest before your freak out.'

'More fish...in sea.' I try eloquently.

'He carries on like this, he's going to wind up shagging sharks. And then he'll be a dickless fish.'

I look at Lee, and she stares back like she didn't just say something ridiculous. It lasts a second, whilst I fear for my sanity, until she chuckles, 'I'm just messing with you.'

'Yeah...bad analogies aren't usually your thing.'

'Oh look how the judgemental artist has returned. Joy. Maybe I liked you better tripping out.'

I pout and wave the water bottle, 'thank you. It really was an accident. And I'm going to shout at Stevo.'

'Why would it be anything other than an accident?' Lee's voice softens.

'Dex thinks I'm doing it for attention.'

Lee takes a deep breath and exhales slowly in a way that means at some point in the near future, Dex is getting a stern talking to. 'There are reasons for everything. That is the least likely. You do what you need to do. But be more careful, please. You're valuable.'

'Valuable?'

'Priceless, even,' Lee grins and puts an arm around my shoulder, 'If only to give that bloody boy a bollocking. Let's plan how we'll punish him for being mean, shall we?'

Chapter Twenty-One

In the end, I couldn't remember which flat was Daniel's. It had seemed so clear to me that morning I'd left his, like I'd know how to find my way back to him no matter what. I'd just finished another day at the gallery, another day where my portfolio sat in the staff cupboard next to the cleaning supplies, gathering dust as Paul winked across at me, showing delegates from whatever country how he had such young, vibrant staff. He didn't like my haircut either.

'It makes you look so much older,' he had said.

All day, I had seen visions of my father, heard the endless criticisms he had given me over the years, the long lectures on the importance of telling the truth, of being upfront and honest with people. If you don't have honesty, you don't have anything. All I could see was images of him fucking faceless women, in the reds of Rothko, in the white tiles on the ceiling. In the surface of the dirty water as I violently squeezed the mop.

I finished my work in half the time, and wandered around central London, unsure where to take shelter. Couldn't go home, I didn't even know whose secrets I was keeping anymore. Who knew what? About Yiayia, about Dad's secrets, Mum's unhappiness, Nicky? I couldn't talk. But that shouldn't be a problem, I was used to keeping things from them, how I felt, what I thought.

I could go to *Baby's*, where Dex would expect banter, and Mona would expect sketches. I could hide at my bus stop, or sit in the bakery in Portobello Road. Instead, I just walked. South and south, down the river, with a watery sunlight warming but not overwhelming me. I put on sunglasses anyway, they made me feel anonymous, like just another Londoner.

Walking felt like action, and I stopped to buy an ice-cream and a packet of cigarettes from the corner shop, the first because I wanted to treat myself, the second because it always seemed like a perfectly destructive way to signify how you feel. I hated smoking. But whenever I felt like crap and I didn't want to drink, or change anything, whenever there was that nervous angry energy, I smoked. It didn't make me feel better.

My feet were leading me, and my brain hadn't panicked yet. All those stories, all those nights at stranger's houses, staying with them, laughing with them, but refusing to sleep with them. How hadn't I been hurt yet? Young woman alone at night in London, bad enough, but the frequency of these strangers, every weekend trying to forget that I had no loan, no job, no future, that I was on a road to a law course, and a life I didn't want. How on earth had I survived, when people get stabbed getting milk from the corner shop, or disappear from clubs? It seemed unfair, like everything else.

I recognised Daniel's road, and after a walking up and down, both to try and remember the building, and decide if I wanted to see him, I just picked a building I liked the look of, and sat on the steps. They were cold, and as I sat there, playing with the lighter, trying not to choke on the cigarette, the cold started to soak through my jeans. How could you be lonely in London? People were everywhere, a stranger, a friend on every corner if you knew how to find them, how to act. Anywhere could be a safe haven, a piece of home to find, like a secret note scattered across the city, hiding pieces of yourself. A particular tree that flowers earlier than all the others in Hyde Park, a basement club under a kebab house, an independent cinema that is always empty during the day. Hide anywhere you like, there will always be people.

'You don't smoke,' a voice said and he'd found me. I knew he would. And I would fight him on it right till the end, because why was he so special? Why should it be him that breaks up my little routine, takes down the rules and regulations I've set for myself so I can't get hurt.? He was fucking with me, he had to be, it was all a game, a joke and if I fell for it, I'd be alone, but it wouldn't have been my choice. I'll have been left behind. Seen for who I really am. Unlovable. He wanted to take away my choice, my barrier. And who was he, anyway?

'You don't know a-'

'-a fucking thing about you, yeah. I've heard that one before.' His voice was harsh, and irritable, and I looked up in surprise. His voice rose, and he leaned close to me, one foot up on the step.

'You're an enigma, right? Someone who can't be understood by an idiot like me? No-one knows you, no-one can possibly comprehend you, you're so special. Well you know what, no-one is that fucked up. And you're here, looking for me. So what's the deal?'

'Maybe I'm not looking for you.' I blew out the smoke and glared at him. I am, I was looking for you, I was! Please, just, see through the bullshit, I can't help it, I'm sorry, I am!

'Ellie.'

'Don't say-'

'ELLIE. That's your name, right? And I will say it however I like. Because I don't know everything about you, but I know enough.'

My bottom lip started to tremble, and I felt my eyes sting, noticing how a vein in his neck became visible and rigid, how his hands moved forcefully, and his eyes seemed darker.

He reached out a hand, and I closed my eyes, not entirely sure what was going to happen, but sure it had probably been a long time coming. I wasn't special, I was anonymous.

His hands were cold, as usual, and he pulled my chin up, traced my jaw. Then I heard as he sat down next to me. I felt the warmth.

'Sometimes, I want to shake you.' He sounded old then, and when I opened my eyes he was wiping his glasses on his shirt. Faded again. Charity shop steal, no doubt.

'I know that you like your tea strong with two sugars. I know you're worried people won't like you, so you keep them at arm's length. I know you cut off all your hair on a whim. I know you try to protect your family from themselves. And I know that you don't know how to exist without being angry, and if nothing's around, you'll be angry at yourself.'

I felt my chest compress, and I knew I was going to cry. Instead, I gasped desperately on the dying cigarette and ended up with a mouthful of ash, and coughed until my eyes watered. His hand reached up and stroked my leg through my jeans, and I couldn't bear to look at his face, only at that hand, moving gently, as if petting an animal that was about to run.

'I know you're lonely,' he said softly, 'I'm lonely too.'

'I know,' I said, afraid to say anything else.

'Were you here looking for me?' He asked, and I knew I had to look at him then, because I heard the smile in his voice. He was hopeful.

I nodded.

'Why?'

'Be-cause...I...want to not be lonely...with you.' I choked it out and screwed my eyes shut.

'That'll do, for now.' He said, and stood up, 'Come on pet, inside. It's the next one over, you were close, though.'

He put a hand to my back to lead me, and I felt suddenly relieved that there weren't any more questions, like he knew he couldn't push me too far. And when I was safe inside that little white room with the green curtains and he'd made me a cup of tea, exactly the way I liked it, I felt safe, I felt like this little piece of home hidden in my city could actually belong to me, I could belong to it.

'My Mama always says you don't know anyone until you know how they take their tea,' I said, breaking the silence, my hands clasped around a cup with a smiling face on, and a chip in the rim. I flicked my tongue through it, and wondered if it was Daniel's favourite cup. If it had a story. If any other girl had sat here and drank tea from it.

'Mine's strong, no sugar.' He offered easily, like I'd asked.

'Good to know.'

'I'm sorry, about before,' he started, sitting down next to me on the bed, 'I just...you don't...I don't get why you push everyone away. You don't need to.'

He needed to shave, and his bristles were lighter than his hair. He wriggled a bit, slurping his tea, and realised he was sitting on his glasses. He grinned at me and rolled his eyes, placing them on the side.

'I lied,' I said, looking straight into his eyes, bright blue that looked darker in the dull-lit room, 'I didn't come here because I don't want to be lonely.'

He nodded for me to continue, a guarded look on his face.

119

'I feel safe here.'

Daniel was silent for a long time after that, but he smiled, and reached for my hand, like he was proud of me. That kind of pissed me off.

I knew somewhere along the line Daniel had been damaged, and had learnt to be alone. He lived alone, he didn't seem to have family, he made decisions for himself. And all of that seemed perfect. But he was lonely.

He grinned and I felt that itching in my stomach again. The corners of my mouth seemed to turn up by themselves, I couldn't help it. He was...beautiful. And smart. And would no doubt break me, leaving my self-esteem shattered, and my promises to myself broken. Unlovable, unloving. He leaned over and kissed me, lingering a moment before, a short, gentle kiss. I could taste his smile.

'Want to watch a movie?' He asked, suddenly like a little kid, 'I've got a terrible selection, mostly from the eighties.'

'Hey, who doesn't love the eighties?' I grinned, and we sat on the floor sorting through the VHS tapes he had bought at charity shops. The quality was fuzzy, irritating and nostalgic. But it felt comforting, it felt like being a kid and getting a new video for Christmas. And I liked the idea that he'd rescued all these little inanimate objects, relics of the past that didn't even really have a value anymore. He didn't give up on them just because something better came along.

When the film finished, he leaned back on the bed, shuffling back, and laying down, staring at the ceiling, 'Come on then,' he said, and patted the space next to him.

I heeled off my trainers, and leaned back, watching as he unbuttoned his shirt, showing a black t-shirt with faded writing underneath. I saw the angry words on his arm again, and reached to touch them. They made me feel like I knew him, like he was kindred.

I turned onto my side, and he switched out the light before following me, not touching me, but paralleling my shape on the bed. I could almost feel his nose against the back of my neck, I could feel his lips as he whispered, 'go on, then.'

The lump was in my throat again, and I started to talk.

'She sings this song, *Kounia Bella,* a lullaby, and she swings me back and forth, and I swear I'm going to fall. But I never do. She always catches me, she's always there...'

I talked until I ran out of words, and I fell asleep to Daniel's encouraging sounds. When I woke at eight am, he was holding my hand. My bag was by the door as ever, waiting for us to get out, go back to what we do, who we are. Instead I fell back asleep, one hand clutching his, and woke up at noon to tea and toast. Somehow, in the morning, I felt free.

Chapter Twenty-Two

'You know I'll never leave you,' his voice wavers over a
fuzzy phone line, and I hear rattling around in the
background.

'I know,' I whisper, 'but are you coming back soon?'

He's waited until our parents are out, and I'm not allowed
to tell them he's called, he knows they won't let him go,
and he won't hang the phone up on them. He's not
rejecting them, he's protecting them. From the shame.
That's what he tells me anyway.

'I can't Ellie, I need to get fixed first,' he sounds so scared,
'It's going to hurt a lot. I know you don't get it, but one
day you will. This thing grabs hold of you and it takes you
over, and all you can do is think about it all the time
because it's so beautiful, and so terrible all at once.'

Nicky's never said that much to me in one go. He talks
with me, but never about the serious things. And I can't
think of anything that would make Nicky run. I hate
Manchester, I blame Manchester for taking him away,
and for the rest of my life I will hate that city, a symbol of
a smoggy disappearance, stopping my brother from
coming home.

'Are you in love?' I ask.

He coughs a laugh down the phone, 'I'm trying to break
up,' he says.

'Kaz, you gettin' in on this mate?' I hear a male voice in
the background.

'El, I gotta go, okay?' he says earnestly, and I hear him
mumble a response to whoever he's with.

'You're gonna come back, Nicky? You're gonna come back,
right?' I'm panicking, and I want my parents to suddenly

walk through the door and run to the phone and make him come back. Lock him up and don't let him out.

'I'll come back, and I'll be better, I promise,' he says, 'and I'll never leave you again.'

He doesn't say goodbye, he just waits until I do before hanging up. Except I don't say goodbye, I say 'see you soon'.

When Mum comes home, I try and let her know that he's alright, that he'll be back soon. She sits me down at the kitchen table with a glass of water, and talks in gentle, dulcet tones, her hand over mine.

'Sweetheart, what do you think is happening with Nicky?' She asks it in a hypothetical way, like it's a subject for discussion in class, or the title of an essay we have to write.

I don't even hesitate because I've spent days thinking about it, and I know what's wrong.

'He's in love, and whoever he's in love with doesn't love him back, and it's making him crazy. So he's gone away to stop being in love. And it's hard to be around happy people when you're trying not to be in love. So he went away to be with other people like him.'

It makes perfect sense, of course, because what else screws people up but love? In all the stories, all the films, it's love that hurts you more than anything else.

'But he'll be back soon, Mama, don't worry.' I pat her hand, and she smiles as her eyes water.

But he doesn't come back, not until the funeral, and then he's gone away again. Every day that passes, I hate this girl Nicky's in love with more and more. I want to find her and pull her hair, scratch her face with my nails. Months and months pass, and it feels like forever. It's a long time where my parents are angry and tired all the time, and my Mama chokes in the night and my Dad smells like brandy but doesn't laugh and offer me any.

When I ask Dad if Nicky's coming back, he tells me not to mention that name in his house. I frown because it's his name too. They're the same person, almost, Nicky's half of Dad. But he walks off before I can say anything. I don't really see Dad anymore, I'm in bed by the time he comes home every night.

Sometimes, when Dad's out, really late at night the phone rings and I hear Mama answer. She says 'hello, hello?' and then she always starts crying. And soon, every night the phone rings, and every night she cries.

Until one day we go to Yiayia's and Nicky's sitting in the kitchen, eating soup, smiling and laughing, even though he's thin and pale. His hair needs cutting, and he's got a fluffy beard growing. He looks like him, and Yiayia places a hand on his shoulder, like she is so proud of him, so sure that everything will be fine.

'Are you not lovesick anymore?' I whisper to him, hovering at his side, whilst Mama makes calls and fusses and rushes about, hands shaking and waving all over the place. Her eyes keep flicking back to Nicky, wary that he might be gone in a blink, she keeps reaching out her hand to him, even from across the room. He pretends not to see, and eats another bowl of soup.

'I'm not sick anymore,' he whispers, and squeezes my hand. His smile is hidden behind his beard, and his teeth are yellow, but I believe him. He never lies to me, he'll never leave me again. He promised.

Chapter Twenty-Three

It was Friday again. I was beginning to dread Fridays. They used to be the symbol of freedom, the beginning of a night that would end up messy, drinking with friends, and making new ones. Not just about the drugs, or the clubbing, but about the ritual.

But without that, my deal with Paul was starting to weigh on me more and more. I walked slowly from where I'd set down my mop and bucket in the corner of the gallery. A bucket full of dirty water looked out of place in the gallery setting. Like you could never imagine things so beautiful needing to be cleaned with everyday objects. But perhaps that was art, darling.

I smiled half-heartedly at Gary the Security Guy. He had to know, and I assumed it was business as usual. 'Off to deal with Head Office bullshit?' Gary asked, sympathetically. He never seemed to judge me on what was going on. I would have. Perhaps because I never showed any enthusiasm, he knew I was just desperate. I wasn't taking advantage, I was simply trying to turn a bad situation into an opportunity.

Perhaps, Gary simply knew the state of the economy, and the art world, and that I was a graduate in a generation that had been promised a future and then kicked out the door. The front step of the real world had grazed our knees and blinded our eyes, until every waitress and barista and bartender was a twenty-something with a 2:1 from a decent university. An entire generation of those art cliches who think it's just a stop-gap job, that someone will give them a break. Everyone hated their job, everyone wanted something more.

I wondered how many of the cleaning girls thought they were artists too, how many Paul had got to service him. How many had gone as far as to sleep with him. I knew I wouldn't. It occurred to me that perhaps the numbness was fallout from the drug use, that the numbness allowed me to do this. Give a disgusting man a quick tug in order to get somewhere, to make something of myself.

Far away in the background, I remembered a version of me that would be shocked at myself, disgusted by the lengths I would go to, how I would compromise myself. How far I would go to to prove Dad wrong.

The self-disgust was coming back, I was starting to remember that I never would have done anything like this. I was being naive, thinking that I could play him at his own game. But he was never going to look at my work, never do anything except pretend that I found him attractive, that he wasn't forcing me, that I wanted him.

I shuffled along the corridors, moving slower and slower at snail pace, tracing my fingertips along the walls. I checked my watch, I was five minutes late. Would he come to find me? Would he scold me? Would he have left already, unsure of how to deal? He'd probably dealt with rejection before, surely, a man like that, in his position. At another time and place, without the threat of law school, before the recession perhaps, I would have registered sexual harassment, found all the girls who worked there before me. I would have buried him.

I opened the office door without knocking. There sat Paul, tugging away violently at himself, breathing hard, whispering angry things to himself. He looked up and saw me, and came in surprise. Sticky fingers, marred desk. And me, clean and untouched. I felt the tight skin around my mouth stretch as I walked out and closed the door behind me.

I walked past Gary who smiled at my wide grin, sure something was up. Sweet relief, all by itself, no drugs, no drink, no escape. And yet a little piece of freedom all by itself.

I went home and started to paint, strange shapes in bold colours. Yellow. Yellow felt happy.

Chapter Twenty-Four

'That's the problem with MDMA, you're constantly searching for that first high all over again. And it's never as good.'

I'm at one of those poncy house parties in Newham, where everyone seems to work in publishing and feel comfortable paying fifteen pounds for a mojito. Everything is black or white, 'fab' or 'an utter disgrace'. Everyone seems to be called Eugenia or Lavinia, and have a double-barrel surname. I have no idea why I'm here, except that Lee went to college with one of the girls who lives here, and now we're surrounded by twats.

'Oh, I don't know, I suppose it depends on the situation,' I say airily to absolutely no-one, and three pairs of eyes suddenly zero in on me.

'You do drugs?' A would-be Teddy Boy who spent twenty minutes trying to convince me that his name was actually Tarquin, raises an eyebrow.

'I'm sorry, I didn't realise you had to pass an exam to get high,' I counter.

'What's the worst thing you've ever done?' Jemima, the mousy girl that Lee knows, asks me.

'What kind of question is that? Shouldn't you ask what the best thing I've ever done is?' I laugh and take a sip of my wine, feeling suddenly superior in this group of what are obviously poseurs.

'Yes, but how much can you take is what they're asking,' a girl called Victoria asks this, seemingly less stuck up, and I like her because she has a lip ring and isn't wearing stilettos. 'Apparently the only interesting thing is how much someone can drink or how many drugs they can take before they die. Because that's a life skill right there.'

I grin at her, and decide we're going to be friends. Maybe one-night friends of the sober variety. I like her, I don't particularly like her choice in company. But then again, I'm in that stupid flat with stupid people drinking stupid wine from plastic cups and trying to seem superior.

'Exactly. It's a better time if you know yourself and what you can handle, and don't push the limit to try and prove you're tough. The most wonderful times I've had have just been laughing and talking with people.' I shrug.

Tarquin scoffs, 'Oh, you're like, well hardcore.'

'You've actually managed to make it sound boring,' Jemima laughs, and I decide Lee has bad taste in people too.

'Well, then I've done my job. Stay in school, kids!' I walk off, and find Victoria following me, brandishing a joint.

'Fancy going outside for a smoke?' she grins.

We sit on a bench down the street, and laugh and do impressions of all the posh kids we can't stand, and after a while, she brandishes a baggie. 'Shall we show them how it's done?'

'I'd rather trash the place,' I roll my eyes, but we go back up, each do a line in the bathroom, and then stand on opposite sides of the room, waiting until we come up to make eye-contact. I zone in and out of a droning conversation with a boy who wants to be a doctor, and a girl who's dad invented something necessary but boring, and eventually, all of my muscles ping into life, and I want to do something, anything. I want to look at the stars, and touch the trees and be anywhere but surrounded by these fake people who create fake beauty because nature doesn't live up to their standards.

'Hey Lee, Victoria?' I shout loudly, 'Wanna go frolic in the park and revel in the beauty of stuff?'

Lee nods, Victoria proclaims 'Hell yes!'

'Why on earth would you do that?' Tarquin chuckled, condescension dripping from his over pronounced chin.

'BECAUSE WE'RE ON DRUGS, LOSER!' Victoria screamed, and we ran giggling down the stairs.

We spent a good few hours, wandering, touching things, looking at the night sky, with Lee laughing or nodding along when necessary, calming us with a touch, cheering us on with giggles.

We made the last tube, and Victoria got off halfway. We hugged goodbye, exclaimed how wonderful the other was, knew we'd never really meet again, and that was fine.

'Always chasing the first time, my arse,' I grumble to Lee, and she just nods.

Chapter Twenty-Five

'You're all in black again, baby' Lee said sadly, as I kissed her cheek. We sat in our corner in The Castle, the first ones there. A little time to ourselves, to catch up, before Dex breezed in, time enough for a quick drink before he disappeared in search of his weekend shag, or Mags waltzed up with her latest crazy story or scatterbrained scheme.

'It's slimming,' I defended, 'It doesn't show dirt. It's perfect for an artist.'

Lee smirked, 'You have paint splatters on your shoes.'

I looked down, and grinned. 'Well, then I'm not all in black, am I?'

I swirled my lemonade around my glass, waiting for the inevitable question. Why aren't you drinking, Ellie? What's going on? Excuses, lies? Do I bring us all down tonight with the truth?

'I have something to tell you,' Lee started, and I felt my stomach drop. No good news ever comes from someone warning you you're about to have a conversation. 'And I really need you to be supportive, no matter what, okay?'

I placed my hands flat on the table. Adopt the brace position. Another secret. Bloody wonderful.

'Okay,' I breathed deep, 'go ahead.'

'I'm in love with Mags.'

Well, it wasn't as bad as I thought. She wasn't running off to join a commune, she hadn't slept with a boy to see what it felt like. She hadn't slept with Dex.

'Okay,' I said, fairly cheerful that it was, for once, one of those nice secrets that girls keep, whisper and giggle about together, and turn into a big drama. A nice secret.

'Okay? Okay!' Her voice squeaked, and I quite liked seeing her off balance, for once. Lee, who was almost a buddhist monk, with her levels of calm, her relaxed way of speaking, her slow, delicate movements. 'What am I meant to do?'

'Well, what do you want to do?' I shrugged, and figured I maybe wasn't being as supportive as I should be, 'How old is Mags anyway?'

'Does that matter?' She frowned.

'Does it matter to you?'

'When did you become a shrink?' She shook her head, and looked around, anticipating Mags' arrival.

We moved in, closer together, as the crowds pushed in on us, and I felt safe, cocooned, hidden. It made me think of when we'd been to girl scouts, when instead of actually going in, we'd get dropped off, then huddle in the church hall rafters, eating cookies and telling secrets. We did that once a week for two years. And then, when we grew up, we traded it for smoking stolen cigarettes at the bottom of her garden, behind the potting shed, sitting on tree stumps under umbrellas, watching as the bottom of our wide-legged jeans got wet.

I watched her, as much my best friend as Dex was, but twice as reliable, holding her wine glass with both hands, like a chalice. She thought I had the answers. Her hair was more blond, almost white, and her eyes looked so much more grey.

I liked that she was demanding something from me, she wanted something, not just my problems. She wanted me to give her advice this time, to stop her from panicking. Lee never panicked. She was scared, and she wanted me to lead her. So, it was love then.

'Do you want to be with her?'

'Yes.' Instantaneous answer.

'Do you think it could work?'

'Ye-es.' Slight stutter.

'Are you going to tell her tonight?'

Lee was warrior-like in her dedication to matters of the heart, all about taking action. You could move slowly, as long as your intentions were direct.

She raised an eyebrow in response.

I patted her hand and smiled, completely truthful, 'this could be a good thing Lee. This could be really, really good.'

I could see she wanted to smile, wanted to believe, to swim in the dreamworld of her crush a little longer, to enjoy the not-knowing. But that part had long since gone if the word Love was being mentioned. Lee didn't Love. She loved her friends, her family, her patients in that home she worked in. She loved the people who needed fixing. And I could see every fear flying through her mind, if Mags didn't feel the same, if she only wanted sex, if she's really straight and the friendship is fucked. That Mags is my boss, and I'd be stuck in the middle, and Dex would come with me, and she'd end up alone.

She held her breath, squeezed my hand and sighed.

'Fuck.'

'Fuck,' I nodded, and clinked my glass with hers.

'So...not drinking?' She asked after a moment of silence.

I fought a frown and held up my glass of coke, 'I'm trying that self-knowledge thing. More to life than being out of it.'

She smiled a little, and I knew she didn't believe me. And she would know, from all those times I called her at two am for the name of a dealer, or wound up on her doorstep after a night out when I had no-where else to run. But she didn't say any of that.

'No vodka in that then?' She stuck out her tongue, and I knew we wouldn't discuss it again.

I rolled my eyes and nudged her in the stomach, and started thinking about how I'd never really offered any advice.

'Hey sweetie, why'd you tell me if you knew I couldn't do anything?'

She frowned at me like it was the most obvious thing in the world, 'You're my best friend, I tell you everything.'

Guilt settled in my mouth, and slipped bitterly down my throat. I rubbed my thumb and forefinger together, and thought about how easy it would be to get rid of that feeling. Half a bottle of cava, a bomb of MD, a shared joint. Two cans of redbull, and then dancing till midnight.

But there was another easy option: I could tell Lee about Yiayia. Trade a happy secret for a sad one. I could tell her everything that was locked inside, about Dad's activities, about Mum wanting to run. About Nicky, locked inside his room, scared of what he'll do if he goes outside.

But I don't, because it's my family. And no matter what happens, however painful it is, however wrong it goes, you don't talk to outsiders about your family. She's my best friend, not my therapist.

I looked across the pub and suddenly everything was louder and closer than it had been. Lovely drunken people laughing, letting the worries of the week slide from them like alcohol, released from their pores tomorrow morning.

I heard a young guy in a group next to us, scowling and waving his pint glass suddenly shout, 'I've got a fucking degree! I locked myself away in third year to get a first! And they won't even hire me in McDonalds!'

'I'll get this round in then, shall I mate?' His friend replied, and the group piled in on a hug, loud and affectionate in the way boys in pubs can be. I smiled, and realised I was one of them, so was Lee. Volunteering three days a week with the mentally ill, and working in a cafe on the weekends, serving fry ups to builders in East London. She's a vegetarian, and she went home on those nights with the smell of dead animal clinging to her. Mags didn't make much on her stall, but enough to survive. She liked to blag bits like that. She did an extra cleaning job a few days a week, because she felt guilty giving her cats own-brand cat food. I never really saw her eat.

It was only Dex who'd committed to a job, full time, something he was good at, foregoing uni life altogether, not constantly aiming for something else, feeling entitled to some sort of future, bigger than the one we had. Maybe he was the smart one.

Mags bounced over through the crowd, already half-pissed and cackling joyfully. I watched as Lee's eyes softened, and figured I must have been blind to miss it. It made complete sense. Of course Lee would love Mags. The universal even-out, providing affection for all the unloved little children, that was Lee. What other people called mistakes, she called character. She loved the little broken parts of people, and they flocked to her to be healed, their beautiful saint who could touch her hand to their foreheads and set them free.

Magda was incorrigible, and her brokenness had long ago become part of her personality. Her flaws were her qualities. She was exciting and unpredictable, halfway to being insane, because she was so brilliant. It could work.

Dex wandered over half an hour later, via a collection of blonds in short skirts. The blonds always annoyed me the most. They were always thin, leggy Amazons, with too much make-up, and supermodel aspirations. He never slept with anyone who could hold a decent conversation, but I suppose that was the point.

'Hello darlings,' Dex kissed me on the cheek, and placed his half-full pint on the table.

'Not drinking?' He raised an eyebrow. He was concerned. I didn't drink on a Friday, and he was worried about me. I wondered if I was a horrible person.

'Not feeling very well,' I shrugged.

'But it's a Friday! Drink through it!'

'I'm on antibiotics,' I smiled, and knew he wouldn't argue. Can't argue with that one...except if I have to make up an illness that they'd give me antibiotics for. My mind went blank. Crap.

'Well, we can all have an end of the night joint, to make up for it,' Mags grinned, and nudged Lee. Lee blushed.

'At the end of the night he'll be shagging some mindless bint in the car park.' I pointed to Dex and took a sip of my drink. He looked almost hurt for a moment, and then that smile returned, more buoyant than before. It was easy to be mean to Dex when he was drunk.

'Oi, I'd at least wait until we got to her place, or mine,' he paused, 'or her car.'

The night droned on, and I started to feel irritable, alone in a sea of drunken conversations, slurring and repetition and laughter for no reason. People making promises, getting excited over things they would never do. They kept repeating the same mindless things, bleating lambs who say their joke again, because they're just so funny. I was starting to resent my friends.

I'd be better off leaving, going home to sit in front of a blank canvas and panic about not painting. Worry about when Mum was going to leave, about that plane ticket I'd found in the cupboard, a one-way ticket to Australia, sitting behind the champagne flutes that were a wedding present from Yiayia. Talk about her plans, not talk about Dad, not talk not talk not talk.

I stood up, gestured towards the toilets, but picked up my coat and bag. I didn't want to have to explain to a bunch of drunkards that I wanted to go, that I didn't want to be there. And they wouldn't understand, or they'd call me names, talk about how I was miserable, wasn't any fun. What was wrong with Ellie, they'd say.

And at the front door, I saw Daniel.

'Hey!' He kissed my cheek, smiling wide, 'I thought you might be here tonight. It's good to see you.'

'Yeah, you too,' I sighed sadly. Because yes, it was lovely to see him, my saviour, my stranger. Mine. Except he was high, coming up. His pupils were huge, cartoon-like, and his lip was jutting in a lazy smile, his eyelids slightly lowered. He looked happy.

He chatted away, introduced a friend standing outside, having a smoke, and I looked at him, pretty boy who'd held me in the dark and listened to my secrets. I didn't want to be around him either.

'You're quiet tonight.' He was tugging at the edge of his t-shirt, the wire rimmed glasses replaced by contacts. He patted at his pockets, hands constantly moving, looking for chewing gum to soothe his automatic chewing. I winced looking at him, feeling his teeth being ground down, and I'd had that feeling so many times before. He brandished the gum in victory, and offered me some, a smile spreading across his face as he started chewing. I knew that feeling, that somehow, chewing is the best thing ever, exactly what you're meant to be doing. Joy in the little things, it was almost a religious experience.

'I'm not anything, I'm just me,' I shrugged, and smiled a little sadly, thinking about how true that was. Without the chemicals, I wasn't very interesting at all. I was average. Daniel's eyes were so dark, the blue had been lost to the dark side, banished to the rim. I was alone in clubland, sober and lonely. No chemical cheat-sheet to happiness.

'Well, I like you just being you,' he smiled and kissed my cheek, and I felt my chest constrict, even though I was in a bad mood, and didn't want to be around drunk and high people.

'But you're not just you right now, are you?' I tried to say it teasingly, to play along and pretend. But really I was just pissed off. It had been my decision to stay sober, to honour some tradition that I wasn't even really a part of. What difference did it make to Yiayia, whether I was drunk or stoned or miserable? She was however many feet under the ground, and not coming back. So why even try?

'I may be buzzing a little, but I'm not a different person,' he said gently, 'I'm just more confident, less quiet. More alive.' His fingers gently rubbed the inside of my wrist, and I couldn't tell if he wanted to comfort me, or the drugs were doing their job, and touching skin felt like the best thing on earth.

'I can't go clubbing tonight, I'm just-' I felt like burst into lonely, tired tears. I was so bored of everything.

'Do you want to go somewhere and just hang out? We could go back to mine and watch a movie, or go sit in a park or-'

'And listen to you commenting on how brilliant the storyline is, or how fucking beautiful the stars are, when all I can see is the shitty normal world? No thanks,' I scoffed.

Anyone else would have walked away, unwilling to sacrifice their hard-earned come-up on someone who refused to be happy. They would have told me to lighten up, loosen up, relax. Stop being such a bitch. But he stood there, and smiled that infuriating smile.

'You're jealous!' He pointed at me.

'Of course I am!'

'You want everyone to be sober when you are.'

'Yes! I want the entire world to be devoid of alcohol and drugs and art and music and clubs and anything that makes anyone happy, because I'm not! Is that okay?' I shouted.

The idiot didn't shout back, or glare, or even stop smiling. He just took my hand, dragged me to the tube, where he sat happily humming to himself until we got to Leicester Square. He then insisted on giving me a piggyback to *Baby's*. He was the first man I've ever let carry me.

So we sat in *Baby's*, in my normal booth, the one that I never really shared with anyone except Dex, and we played noughts and crosses, and hangman. He tried to share an ice cream with me, although he had no appetite. And we talked. About nothing, about things that would still be true after the comedown. How he thought Spaced was the best thing to have ever been on TV, how he liked John Woo films, and hated reality TV. And then the true things, about how he lived in a little village up north, how his mum moved them from place to place, never settling. How he had a girlfriend who wanted to get married when they were fifteen, and how he ran away to London. The real things, I supposed. The bits that stopped him being my stranger, and turned him into my something else. And it felt right.

Mona smiled as she brought over endless cups of coffee, because I wasn't there with Dex. Daniel smiled because he couldn't help it. And I smiled. Because.

Chapter Twenty-Six

I stand on the edge of the road, looking out at the sea. We're in Cyprus, and I've left my family sitting in the restaurant we come to almost every night, bloated and tired from the rich food and the endless wine. The little taverna is red brick, open air, with columns at the front. It's called *The Icarus* and I hate the cliche of it, the lack of subtlety. It sits on a narrow road, houses and restaurants to one side, and the sea on the other. There is no railing along the road, and every time Dad drives, I'm terrified we'll skid into the sea and drown. I stand as close to the edge as I can bear, in between parked cars, no street lights, hidden in the darkness.

I love hearing the sea when I can't see it. It's dark and viscous, and I can't tell where it ends and the night begins. The sea reflects the dark, and the moon isn't around. I feel gloriously alone. I can still hear the occasional conversation, raised voices, clinked glasses from the restaurant. Dad will be out soon, scold me for wandering off, wanting an explanation. And I don't have one.

I peer over the edge, notice how it's smooth like a cliff face, only just high enough to be scary. Who knows how deep the water goes? It sloshes, and I imagine if I fell, I'd be covered in oil, drowning in thick liquid that would coat my lungs and choke me. It wouldn't be salty, it would be like chocolate, dark and bitter.

I lean forward, and shuffle my feet to the edge. I take a deep breath, and shift my centre of gravity towards the dark. Automatically, my body tingles, my heart thumps and I throw myself backwards in self-preservation. As I stand shaking, I feel myself drowning, feel myself leave my body, becoming ether, becoming particles. Breathing once more and then nothing. Gone. Now I lay me down to sleep.

It happens every now and then, when I have the ridiculous urge to turn into oncoming traffic, to step out in the road without looking, stand on the edge of a balcony ten stories up. I'd never do it, but my body doesn't know that. It likes to be reminded. It makes me feel alive. Afraid and trembling, and completely alive.

I love to watch the sea in the dark, it feels like it holds secrets. I put my arms around myself, rubbing my shoulders for something to do, letting my heart settle back into it's natural rhythm. I hear my mother wonder where I am, and prepare myself to return, knowing I'll be flushed and shaking, full of adrenaline.

But I can't leave the sea. During the day, it's a different thing, it's a natural, friendly thing, children bobbing in it, reflecting sunlight like smiles. You can sit in it forever, waves lapping at your ankles like eager puppies. You can float with your eyes closed, sure that you're surrounded by this beautiful blueness, an honest reflection of the sky.

At night, it's different, like it's hiding a different world, underneath. Not fish and crustaceans, or buried ships, but the dead, wandering in and among the algae. The sea is made of the dead, made of us, our remains, our chemicals. It takes our dreams and secrets and washes them away. Stores our sins in the sound of the waves.

Years from now, at art school, I will try to paint the sea as I see it now, this dark sloshing, this endlessly beautiful destructive thing, but I won't be able to find the right colour. The blues will look too happy, too honest with sparkling jades and seductive royals, never serious enough. My tutor, an intense woman who makes art a science will tell me that the Ancient Greeks had no word for blue, that Homer described it in his writings as 'wine dark' in lieu of anything else. I paint my sea in various plums, and my teacher says my penchant for taking things literally inhibits my work.

But for now, the darkness irritates me with its immunity. I want to capture it, keep it close, help remind my heart to flutter. Instead, it slips from my fingertips, never leaving a remainder.

Chapter Twenty-Seven

'Mama?' I called out, opening the front door. I'd become convinced every time I returned home that she'd be gone, there'd just be a note on the table saying 'Off to have adventures, toodles!'

I'd watched her over the weeks, every time Dad called to say he'd be late, every time he disappeared for hours on Sunday to get his car washed, or drove to the park so he could go walking. Her mouth would twitch slightly, the briefest of tenses, then the acceptance. Her eyes would shift downwards, then she looked up eyes bright as ever, supportive and adoring.

'His mother's just died,' she would say over and over again, 'It's so hard for him, I know. When my father died, all I wanted to do was hide from the world.'

But you didn't, I wanted to tell her, *you were there for us, you looked after everybody.*

I walked into the kitchen, and she was sitting at the table with a cup of tea, staring at the plane ticket. So, this was it.

'I used to go away by myself, all the time, when I was young,' she smiled up at me tiredly, and tucked a strand of hair behind her ear. It looked like there were a few lines of grey in it now, the red washed into mouse brown. 'I used to just talk to people, make friends easily. Laugh a lot.'

She tapped her nails on the teacup, frowning at it, 'I'm sure back then, I never used to feel this shit about myself.'

'He's done it to you,' I said before I could help myself, and my mother's smile was just like a mother's should be; like she knew better.

'Your dad, you mean?' Her mouth twitched, 'That's quite a thing to blame someone for, Ellie, years of unhappiness. Being responsible for how another person is? And if he's made me like this, I've made him whoever he is, doing whatever he does.'

Her voice became very small, and her smile was lost as she looked at me, 'And I'm not quite ready for that.'

I sat down at the table with her, the kitchen table that had been there since I could remember, the gloss of the wood worn away from hot drinks, scissors, candlewax that had to be chipped off. The writing on thin paper so that the words were carved into the table underneath. I traced the soft indentations with my fingertips.

'So, where to?' I gestured to the plane ticket, making my voice light and excited, 'Don't tell me South America, if I'm not allowed to go there, then you can't beat me to it.'

'Oh actually,' she cleared her throat, 'I traded in the ticket for my little trip, got a weekend in Venice instead, for me and your dad.'

'Oh.'

'Yeah.'

She stood, and reached behind the coffee pot, shaking free another squashed pack of cigarettes.

'So, no backpacking, huh? No big alone adventures?' I tried not to sound disappointed.

She smiled sadly, 'Let's be realistic for a minute, darling. I'm accustomed to a certain way of life, aren't I? Thirty years of saving, and four star hotels, and no longer having to worry about whether I can afford to eat in a certain restaurant, I'm going to go backpacking? At my age? People would laugh, God, think what they'd say about me!'

'Fuck what people say.'

'Ellie,' she sighed, 'I don't expect you to understand, you're young, you've got everything open to you. Just trust me on this, okay? I'm better off sticking with what I know.'

She turned on the hob, and leaned over the flame to light her cigarette, her face dangerously close, and she closed her eyes with the heat of it. She coughed slightly on the exhale.

'I really ought to quit,' she sighed.

'But you don't smoke, Mama.' I said, and she saluted me with the cigarette.

'I'm doing the right thing, for all of us,' she smiled, bright and honest, her eyes stinging and watering at the smoke that surrounded her.

'Whatever you say, Mama,' I replied, taking one of the cigarettes she offered, and lighting it from hers so she wouldn't be alone.

Chapter Twenty-Eight

I'm too young to understand when Mum's dad dies. I'm held in a lot of people's arms, they pass me around like a parcel, taking off layers and rewrapping me when they think I'm cold. We stand around the graveside in a small village in Ireland that I never return to, and it's grey and windy, but doesn't rain. People come and go with those soft voices that sound just like my Mama's.

The adults are talking about a wake, about an open coffin and his eyes staring out. My mother is young and beautiful, her hair bright red, so much more alive than all those people who come to pay respects.

Nicky takes my hand, a guiding force, and stands behind Mum. We're her protectors, we stop bad things happening.

'Mama's gonna be sad, Ellie, okay?'

'I know!' I insist, because I'm at that age where I pretend I know anything that anyone tells me.

My father kneels down beside me and tells me to be a good girl. 'We've got to be really quiet, *kori-mou,* that's what this is about, we're quiet and still. It's like musical statues.'

'Or sleeping lions!' I exclaim, and watch my mother's mouth twitch.

The priest has a kind voice and furrows in his forehead that make him look like a wax sculpture. He smiles at me, and continues a long boring sermon about God. I hear the word 'Amen' and know to put my hands together and look like I'm praying.

We always have to pray before meals at school, so I think of school dinners when I'm bowing my head. Chips dipped in custard. Lumpy mash. Gravy with skin so it wobbles in the bowl. Whenever I pray I think of food. Not of the dead stranger who was my mama's daddy. I never met him, and I think he must have been a mean man for my mummy to run away from him and never go back.

When we go back to the house, I wander around the dusty bookshelves, and eventually me and Nicky sit under the dining room table so no-one can see us. We see old shuffling feet in brown shoes and beige tights. Men who get louder as the night goes on. And singing, these beautiful songs that go on for ever about wars and loves they lost but never stopped thinking about. Mostly I just listen to how the words sound, how their voices warble up the notes, like birds.

We fly home the next day, and Daddy takes us out for ice cream so Mama has time to 'do all her bits and pieces'. It's how he tells us we're in the way. We get Mr Whippy ice cream cones, and walk round the park, and when we get home, Mum hugs us and kisses us and sends us to bed. I hear my dad turning on the TV and the give of the leather sofa as he watches the football re-runs. I hear as my mother drags her feet up the stairs, the slow, soft thumps. I hear the running of the water, the brushing of teeth. Light off in the bathroom, light on in the hallway. Light on in the bedroom, light off in the hallway. Closed door.

And then I hear this choking sound. Coughing, squeaking, gasp. I tiptoe to the door and push it open slowly. Mum is sat on the floor at the foot of the bed, only partially visible in the dull light. She smiles widely when she sees me, but her eyes are red and watery. She welcomes me with her arms, and brushes my hair back.

'What is it darling, can't sleep?'

I shake my head. I want to tell her I missed her, that I'm sad she's sad. That she can share my Daddy now she doesn't have one any more. But I'm scared.

She lifts a small glass of whisky to her lips and the smell makes me feel sick. It's like medicine, like brandy, all those summers in Cyprus where the men drink and smoke. But it's worse somehow because it smells like tears and sweat and that strange singing we heard from under the table.

'The only land we inherit is three by five,' she says into my hair, 'so it's good to be important, but it's better to be kind.'

I freeze in her arms because I don't know what she means, I don't know what she wants me to do. So I just sit there in her arms and drift away as she strokes my hair. When I feel her shuddering, and hear those horrid little gasps that sound like she's drowning, I clamp my eyes shut tight, and pretend that I'm asleep.

When I wake up the next morning, Mama's made pancakes, singing as she flips them. And I wonder how everyone forgets to be sad so quickly.

Chapter Twenty-Nine

It's Bestival, and I can't even remember my own name. Everyone else did Reading or Leeds or Glasto, but I waited, entirely sure that something better was out there. It was Mags' idea, and I loved that she wasn't the least bit bothered that she was older than the rest of us. This was her style, her life. She drove me and Dex down in her VW camper, and we pitched up right beside her. She disappeared for a good amount of time that weekend. Occasionally we'd see her at the front of a crowd, or talking quietly to the tarot readers in the healing fields. Mags' people.

The first thing we do to reward ourselves for not only putting up our tent, but for finding Lee and her friend Lola, is to sit and have a joint and a cider, and plan out our time. The smell of weed seems to be ignored by every hippie, and attract every stressed out, something-to-prove kid around.

Her name is Bella, and she does not stop talking. She gabs on and on with that wide red mouth, her little eyes blinking incessantly. She talks about art and politics and The Game of Survival That Is Life, and lots of other shit that makes me want to muffle her with a damp sleeping bag. I start grinding my teeth, and Lee pats my back gently, throwing me worried glances every now and then.

'Well, we've been here a while, we should go check out the stages and stuff,' I say pointedly, but Dex is staring back at me with a look I recognise. Part of it is pure six-year-old, when I tried to bully him into giving me his boomerang. The other is the same face he pulls every time he's getting somewhere with a girl and I get in the way. His arm is already around Marnie, a poor sweet thing who doesn't really know what to do with his affection.

She's not as stupid as the usuals, and she's pretty and studying something like marine biology, and can talk in full sentences, so mostly I just pity her, and hope Dex isn't expecting too much. That leaves Rowan, who's said nothing for the last hour. He's nodded, he's shrugged, he's ruffled his hair and he's made an exasperated noise. But he's very good at rolling joints, so I don't actively dislike him.

'Urgh, movement. Can't we just stay here and chat?' Bella's voice booms, and seeing as she's gesturing with a joint made from my weed, I think maybe no, we can't stay here and listen to you whilst you chat about things that make my head explode. Thanks, though.

Of course, I say 'Fine, whatever, I'm going to wander.'

Lee and Lola decide to come with, Dex stays with the girls, of course, and Rowan throws his head back and forth like a horse trying to signal something.

'You coming?' I ask.

He brays a little and shrugs, getting up. We don't say much, stay close together, wandering through people and stalls and music until everything closes in, and I feel dopey and happy, and all I can think is a cup of tea on Mags' stove, and curled up like kittens in our tent full of blankets and cushions sounds like heaven. Except Dex will be banging someone tonight. I sincerely doubt it will be Marnie, but it'll be someone. And he better not be in my tent whilst he does it.

We reach a tent where slam poets are battling. There's beatboxing and hip hop and people are so hyped up, cheering on in surprise and shock at how much a word can convey that I feel alive and in awe. I want to make art like that. I want to express like that. I see them in colours, on canvas in my mind's eye, and I want to take a picture so I can paint them at home. I bring out a

151

notepad, and sketch briefly, enough to capture the feeling, if not the vision. The beginning of a new series of work that I'll start at university, and still not be done with in thirty years, callled 'Broken Poet'. I paint artists in the way they least want to be seen; vulnerable, normal, uninteresting, angry. Alive. Not on paper or on a wall, but living, breathing art. My tutor loves it, my friends hate it. And it traces back to the festival.

'Sorry I haven't said much,' a voice appears in my ear, shocking me from the sketch. It's Rowan.

I shrug, 'You can do what you like.'

I can hear him grin in my ear, and his cheek brushes against my hair, 'I'm trippin' balls here. Seriously, it's amazing. Acid!'

I turn to face him, tilt my head to the side and consider him. 'Isn't that a bit cliche?'

He shrugs again, but grins, 'I'm just making myself happy. I'm not hurting anyone. Anyway, I didn't want to freak you out, so I was just...ya know...being. And then I thought maybe I was freaking everyone out by not saying anything. So I thought I would. Say something, I mean.'

He's actually quite pretty, once he pushes the dirty blond curls away from his face. His smile splits his face, and his lip ring twitches.

'Thanks, for being so thoughtful. Is it too distracting to talk, then?' We edge further back from the stage so we can hear one another, and he smiles again.

'Nah, just...Bella.'

That smile I share in. I just watch him watching things for a while, trying to guess what he's seeing, maybe even allowing my eyes to make shapes in the way I imagine an acid brain does. He doesn't stand around pointing at things or acting strangely, he just looks at everything with a childlike wonder. When we walk outside and look up at the stars, he grabs my hand and gasps. I fall a little bit in love with him in that moment.

'Did you want to try? No pressure,' he shrugs again. Nothing with Rowan could possibly be pressured, I realise.

'You know, I'm really okay. I don't think I need to,' I feel like a grown-up for a brief minute, but the truth is, I'm scared of what my brain will bring up. Ecstasy is different, pure chemical balance and imbalance. Nothing pressing on your nerve endings to make you see things. And I can imagine the sorts of things I'd see. Weird gurning faces, Nicky's emaciated form running away, like a skeleton in those nightmares I used to have when he first came home, until I couldn't even sit next to him at dinner. The visions of his face half eaten away by maggots or decay. No, I don't want to know what my brain can create.

Rowan shrugs, and keeps holding my hand.

I wake up that morning to Dex scrabbling into the tent with all the finesse of a drunken jungle cat. It's starting to get light, but it's stuffy and dry, and there's still many more hours of sleep to be had. I see Lee's hair poking out from her sleeping bag, Lola's pink-tipped hair splayed across a pillow she's curled around in the corner.

Dex tries to wriggle into his sleeping bag, and falls down beside me, squishing me into the side of the tent. I growl a little, but don't want to wake the others. Just as he's finally still, the shouting starts.

'What did you fucking do, you whore?'

'Nothing, we didn't do anything!' The voices sound Essex, but that's an over-tired guess.

'He was plying you with drinks all night! He was clearly up to something!'

'Becky, please!' The girl whines, still slurring, 'I feel sick!'

'Of course you do! You can't just bring some fucking guy back and shag him whilst I'm in the tent asleep! That's a fucking awful thing to do!' She's screaming at her friend, and as annoying as she is, I have to agree with her. And then I look at Dex, still as anything, not even breathing audibly. Of course.

'I didn't have sex with him!'

'Your shorts are open.' Becky seems to win with that remark, and she's joined by a boy, who seems to agree with her, 'Yeah Jen, you're a right fucking state.'

'I didn't have sex with him!'

The boy starts up, 'Well, I looked in the tent and saw a hand! A fucking hand! And it was around a penis! So either you were jacking him off or he was doing it himself, with you and Becky in the tent!' He starts laughing, and I can't tell whether to laugh or hit Dex.

I roll over and whisper, 'You're a fucking moron, Fabian.'

He sighs, 'I know,' and wriggles his arms free so he can put them around me.

'Oi,' I stage whisper, 'I don't know where those hands have been!'

He briefly squeezes me, then lets go, and I curl up even smaller so that I don't miss his warmth.

Bella, Rowan and a decidedly smitten Marnie return the next day, and hang around and smoke our weed and drink our beer. Rowan zones out, Marnie smiles and Bella talks. I spend most of my time away from the tent. We party till four am. The morning after that, they come back again. I spend all day away from the tent and everyone

154

else, becoming a stranger in the crowds, the same way I've been feeling safe my entire life.

I decide that I only really want two types of friends; the enduring, loving wonderful imperfect forever friends, who I never doubt, always question and can say anything to. And the one night friends, who are everything for a night, and then they're gone. Drunk or not, those one-night friends become week long friends, and they lose their sparkle quickly, until I can't stand people at all.

Chapter Thirty

There are nights that I sleep in the Big Old House when she tucks me up in a big bed where the mattress is lumpy and the sheets are too tight, and I ask her to tell me a story. The whole house smells like olive oil and cookery, the wind taps on the thin windows, and she brushes back my hair with a firm hand, and asks what story I'd like to hear. I always ask for the same one.

'Tell me about Persephone,' I demand, trying to say the name the way she says it. I wriggle down under the ancient scratchy covers, clutching an apple or orange, some piece of fruit I haven't found a way to discard yet.

'Again, dahlink?' She smiles in that gentle way that makes me think of Mama. Mama and Daddy went out tonight, all looking pretty and smart with their big smiles, and heavy coats. Mum's hair was bright, and she had diamonds in her ears. I love it when they look happy, even if it means that Nicky gets to go to a friend's and I have to sleep in the Big Old House.

'Okay, Persephone beautiful daughter of Dimitra. Dimitra is nature, she touch trees and flowers and they...bloom. They go along together, mama and *kori,* walk in nature. They live happy.

'One day, Persephone go by herself, alone. She go to the water and she never be alone before. She hear her breath, hear sound of quiet. She talk to water to hear her voice. And then, a God comes.'

I always wriggle at this point, fluff my pillows, pretend I'm doing something to hide the delicious thrill as my skin tingles. The dark prince appears.

'He name Hades, and he God of the dead. He show spirits the way to afterlife. And he see Persephone, most beautiful, and he steal her away, underground.'

'But she was a goddess too, Yiayia!' I exclaim, as I always do, 'why didn't she run away, escape?'

'Because she...she useful, *kori*. She give the spirits hope, and she see he kind to the dead. So she marry him and become Queen of the underground. And the spirits so happy to see such beautiful face when they die.

'But Dimitra, she miss her *kori* very much. She walk the world, shouting 'kori, kori' but she never find her. So she punish the land and the people. She make flowers die, she make storms, and it cold and rain and dark. She hurt, so the world hurt.'

I always check outside now, check the weather. Is Dimitra angry today? Will she take it out on me. Whenever I see a storm, I love to sit at the window and watch, feeling sorry for Dimitra, because she must be really missing her daughter that night. The window rattles, and I see the tree swaying outside in the darkness. A mother's despair.

'And the people, they die, so they ask the Gods, they pray. They say we do everything, we worship, we pray, we love you, why you no love us? So, the Gods make a deal, to save the people. Persephone go to mama half the year, and husband other half. So we have season. Her family in light, love in the dark. This is always.'

'What does that mean? Even humans?'

'Dahlink, is hard explain.' She runs her fingers through my hair, and her face wrinkles as she smiles. She never dyes her hair, or puts on make-up, she's happy to age, happy to meet Hades one day.

'Hades doesn't take people soon, does he Yiayia? Will he come get me?' I feel stupid for asking, a silly little girl.

'*Kori-mou* don't be silly billy!' She taps my leg, pulls up the covers and turns out the light. She pauses briefly in the doorway, the light making her no more than a dark, wide figure.

'Yiayia! Why doesn't Persephone leave Hades? He's King of the Dead!'

'Because sometimes, dahlink, when you come from light, from happy and beautiful all time, you want dark. Dark and quiet and sad. And because he her husband. You don't leave your husband.'

She smiles briefly, and I hear her clump downstairs, where Pappou is calling for her. As I fall asleep, I dream I am Persephone, and I dance in the sunlight, and climb the trees, and everything I touch flowers and bursts into life. I see Hades appear as a beautiful man, destined to be sad, to be a deathly king. And I wonder if he really stole her away, or if she ran to him. If the sunlight was just too much to bear.

Chapter Thirty-One

He looks intimidating, but my drug-addled brain senses a sweetness. He says his name is Marcus, and he's mid-thirties. Dark skin, bright white teeth and a booming laugh. He's sweating constantly, moving, bouncing in time with the bass, and every now and then he clicks his jaw. There's a delicious dangerousness about him, and whilst I know I'm not attracted, there's something attractive there.

Maybe that he opens his coat, and there's a different drug in every pocket. Night sorted, nothing to worry about. Yes, a woman should be safe, but she should also be practical.

I see Dex across the club, leaning into the space of some sweet young blond thing, all bubblegum and tattoos, and he waves. I raise an eyebrow and grin.

'Your boyfriend, love?' Marcus' voice takes on an edge, but he's smiling and dancing all the same.

'Nah, never.' I put on a more 'London' voice. I'm street, I'm cool, I'm doing what all the cool fucked-up teenagers do.

'Good, because I've got a present for you,' his hand clasps mine, and I feel the baggie, warm and sticky in my palm, 'go to the toilet. I'll be here.'

'Cheers Marcus!' I say, kissing him on the cheek, sweetly surprised by how nice strangers can be, except I'm not, because I'm high as anything, and everyone's wonderful, and everything's safe. The dingy toilets with scribbled epitaphs like 'Latoya loves Big Dwayne foreva' become home to poetry of our generation. The hand dryers are a mystery, and possibly, an environmental phenomenon. The music is nothing but bass, and I nod along, bracing my foot against the stall door because the lock was broken years ago. I gum the powder, a small part of myself not wanting to snort, because who knows what he's given me. Sensible Ellie, good girl. I don't think of my parents or friends, or anyone at all. I think about the cloud of pink light that's lifting inside my rib cage, and how my heart makes music, and how Marcus seems like a more interesting one-night friend than usual. He's not a Dexter, not at all.

I bound back out, widening my eyes for the sheer joy of feeling my eyelids stretch.

'You good, little darling?' He's shouting in my ear, and I focus on his clothing, his dark jeans and paisley shirt and wonder what the hell he's even doing here. But he laughs, and that makes him beautiful.

We dance, and he doesn't touch me, occasionally grabs a sweaty hand with his own to spin me round, but beyond that, it's fine. We sit outside and smoke, talking about all those things that seem important. Fuck the Man, NHS, the death of communication, what TV we've seen, why TV is shit. We spurt pointless words for what feels like a night, bullet after bullet of engaging thought that makes the world seem small but endlessly fascinating. We are alive, and golden, and everything else is mess.

'Back to mine?'

This is the question it hinges on, and it helps that he gives me a line of coke before I make my decision on whether or not to face the nightbus to Hackney. Dexter is nowhere to be seen, and won't answer his phone, already balls-deep in some pointless bint no doubt, so I shrug and say 'okay'.

I rest my head on his sweat soaked shoulder on the bus home, and we tap out rhythms on each other's knees. My purple bag rests at my feet.

I stop moving for a second, close my eyes, feel the jolt of the bus, and try not to fall apart. It's fine as long as I keep clicking my fingers or twitching my wrist. I don't shudder when he touches my neck with his sticky hands. When he whispers things I don't understand into my ear. As long as I focus on how I feel happy and can't feel anything else, then it's all fine and wonderful and we're just one-night friends.

'We can be curled up in my bed, all warm. It'll be nice,' he smiles, and I try not to notice how red his eyes are, or my grey reflection in the bus windows, calling me a moron.

'Why don't we go dance somewhere else?' I hear my voice raise an octave.

'I don't want to dance anymore, darling.'

'Oh.'

My phone rings, and I grab at it. Dex. 'Where the fuck did you disappear to?' His voice is irritated, if not frantic.

'Oh, don't act like this a new thing, jeez.' I roll my eyes at Marcus.

'Did you go off with that guy?'

'Yes. Are you still inside that girl, or were you polite enough to pull out before you called me?' Coke always makes me aggressive, I don't know why I bother.

'I'm going to pretend that's whatever stupid shit you've snorted talking. Where are you?' Dex always seemed to sober up after a drunken shag. Better than coffee.

'On a nightbus to Hackney.'

At that point, Marcus took the phone, 'Look, loverboy, she doesn't want to talk to you, okay? She's with me. Don't call again.' He hangs up, clicks his jaw and throws the phone at me.

'That was rude,' I say quietly, because his hand is twitching and I'm starting to remember that I only do this when it feels right, and nothing feels right.

'Shut the fuck up. What did you take that call for?'

Oh, shit.

'He's my friend, he was worried about me.'

'Well, he shouldn't be, you're with me.' Marcus' eyes glare at me, and I realise it's time to get my London hat on. Escape Plan A.

'You're absolutely right, I'm so sorry. It was very rude of me to take that call. It won't happen again.' I smile, stroke his hand and try not to vomit. The girl in front of us dings the bell, and I wait until the bus stops. Marcus is chatting away, happy now that I've apologised for nothing, (and boy, do I know that type) and I pretend to stretch, before grabbing my purple bag and jumping off the bus. The doors close behind me and he's hollering for the bus to stop. It won't, but I run anyway.

East London. Bleh. I walk for half an hour, the coke giving me the extra kick, pulling my hoodie on with the hood up, looking like someone people should be scared of. I get a nightbus to Waterloo, then get a train. Then I get a cab. I text Dexter with one word. Sorry.

He opens his front door and lets me get into bed with him. I leave before he wakes up.

Chapter Thirty-Two

Another Friday at the gallery. Paul. All I ever seemed to do was drag around a mop and bucket in surprise and disgust, counting down the seconds till Friday afternoon. The physical sick feeling had started up again, and I wondered if Paul would take a note from my mother.

Dear Mr Butler, Ellie is not feeling well today. Please allow her to leave work early so she is not faced with the dire situation of whether or not to please you sexually. Yours sincerely, Mrs Kazakis.

Somehow, I didn't think it would work.

I kept telling myself that I was stupid; how on earth had I survived the situation that long, with that man? Questioning how I hadn't projectile vomited across his lap. Maybe that would work. How did I even start this? Determination and numbness, I supposed. Perhaps I could blame the comedown, the deadened sensation receptors, letting me do things I couldn't believe I could do. Maybe I was just power hungry, blind and proud. Not proud enough to say 'no', but too proud to run home and tell my family I'd failed.

I started the trail to Paul's office, completely sure that I should tell him to go to hell, threaten him, belittle him, and storm out.

'Hey, Ellie,' Gary the Security Guard smiled at me, 'there's a guy at the front desk waiting for you.'

Gary's smile seemed genuine, as always, but there was something else there. A sideways tilt of the head, asking a question. Are you going to stop now, Ellie? Are you going to give up, sweetheart? You've done your time now, time to go. He nodded slowly with that sage kind of wisdom of his, and winked.

'Tell him I'll be right down, just got to sort some stuff out,' I said.

'Good for you, love,' he nodded, and patted my shoulder briefly before walking away. For some reason that made me want to cry.

I trudged down the corridor, that long endless white walkway, and smiled my farewells to the paintings. I've seen you when the crowds are gone, I know you, I love you. Goodbye.

I didn't knock on Paul's door, just pushed it open with as much force as I could manage. Do it fast, get out quickly. Done. Over.

'Ellie!' I hated, hated, hated when he said my name. His pinstripe trousers were already unzipped, his flaccid dick on display through the glass desk. He gestured towards himself in a hilarious motion, as if to say: well, here it is, what are you waiting for?

I wanted to tell him that I hated him. That he was an A-grade wanker who took advantage of young people with dreams and ambition, angling them into immoral situations. That he was old, and out of touch, and that no-one would even look at him, let alone touch him, if it wasn't a stepping stone to get to where they wanted. But I knew it was my fault. That I would do anything, and you can't blame the person who takes advantage of that.

'Paul, listen. I'm quitting.'

He frowned, then smiled, 'And why on earth would you do that?' He shook his head like I was a silly girl having a bit of a tantrum. His face assumed a fatherly concern.

'This really isn't what I want my life to be, to be honest. It's nothing personal, I just don't want to do this anymore.' I smiled openly at him, whilst he

164

surreptitiously tucked himself back into his trousers. The slip of the zip was his only response.

'So, thanks for everything,' I said, ready to leave.

'Now, Ellie,' He started, 'don't be silly sweetheart, this is a great opportunity you're turning down here. You've got talent, you could go places.'

'I know, that's what I'm trying to do. And you've never seen my work, Paul, so as far as I can tell, my chances for advancement are nothing to do with my artistic skills.'

'I-uh...hmmm.' His sounds of confusion were not dissimilar to his sounds of excitement.

'Let's keep it simple,' I held out my hand, 'Thanks for everything, best of luck.'

He shook my hand, furrowed brow, not entirely sure what was happening. Had no-one ever rejected him before, I wondered. Perhaps he thought I was doing those things because I wanted to, it had nothing to do with a career? Perhaps he was a lonely old man who was not my responsibility.

I closed the door gently behind me, and strode down that corridor for the last time. Freedom. Except freedom felt a lot like taking a chance on something with no future, no prospects. Freedom sounded like letting Dad win, like however many years of law school. But even so, doing the right thing for once had a nice light feel about it.

I didn't look at the paintings as I left, abandoning them to another young cleaner/artist who would love them and let her boss use her.

I reached the ground floor, ruffling my hair, as Gary and Daniel stood chatting.

'Bonnie,' he nodded.

'Clyde.'

'Feel better?' He asked, rubbing the base of my spine in small circles. What he was asking was 'did you do it, did you end it, are you mine, just mine?' And all I wanted to do was say 'yes' over and over again.

'I feel wonderful. That freedom of joining the rest of the unemployed. Exhilarating,' I grinned as we waved goodbye to Gary.

'Ready to get the hell out?' He lead me through the glass doors, and outside, where the air was cool, and the evening quiet.

'What a hero,' I laughed at him, 'aren't we meant to ride off into the sunset in a really cute Cadillac or something?'

He shrugged and adjusted his glasses as his grasped my hand.

'I've got an Oyster Card, and a warm can of Stella in my pocket. That do?'

'Perfect,' I said.

Chapter Thirty-Three

'*Pappasmou...*' She stops and clears her throat, and remembers to resume in English. 'My father, he hide up there, when Turks come.'

She points up to the highest point of the mountain, way above her village, past the women sitting outside making lace, past the donkeys loaded with chubby children. The tourists wander around with their oversized cameras, and white stripes of sunblock on their noses, getting sucked into conversation with the locals, who will give them a good deal on silver jewellery. Oh *nai, nai kombaro,* finest on the island. You try, for your pretty wife*, nai?*

'Why did the Turks come, Yiayia?' Gali asks, 'What did they want?'

'*Panayia,* dahlinks, you know what happen? Every person in village go hide in the *monastiri.* And when they bomb, the people hide in caves. Like animal.' Her voice shakes with anger, with disgust, and I repeat the words my father still uses when he drives through Haringey or Finsbury Park: '*Vromo tursky*'. Dirty Turks.

'*Oki*, kori-mou. You don't hate. Hate no help, *katalaves?*' But her eyes return to the mountain top.

Theo Christos nods, solemn. 'They defaced all the icons in the church, burnt them down, slashed them, to chip away the gold in the paint.' His dark eyebrows are furrowed, and he suddenly looks very big, very angry.

'Both side blame, Christos. Always war, always want more. We used to live together once, *ola mazi.* Always big men, big plan. Why no be happy?' Yiayia starts whispering to herself in Greek and we look up to her, lost and scared. How could people live in caves? What about food and drink? My mind is lost with where they put the toilets, and how many people there were and what it smelled like.

She shakes her head and drops of sweat run down from her temple, so she takes us by the hand and walks us down narrow streets until we reach the taverna. The taverna we always go to, the only one in the village, with the fresh flowers on the veranda, and average food. A pretty view with large glasses of fresh orange juice. My Cyprus. The years will pass, more shops and tavernas will open, more tourists will come. A hotel, an art gallery. But every year after, me and Gali will sit there holding hands as we looked up to the top of the mountain, imagining Turks as big, dark warriors who come in the night with fire and knives.

We stay at Yiayia's sister's house; my parents, Gali's parents, Yiayia. Pappou has already gone to his own village, higher up the mountain, to see his own family. He takes Nicky to walk amongst his orange groves, to touch the land, and speak to strangers. They will return before we leave, and Pappou will be kinder, smiling. Nicky will scowl and call everyone *bello blasmas*. Stupid, stupid people.

That night me and Gali have nightmares, visions of men in dark clothes, of scared faces praising God. We imagine the smell of candles in the church.

Gali whispers, 'Do you think the Turks will get us?'

'Why would they want us?'

I see her outline in the dark, her face scarily white and serious. I want Nicky back, I miss Nicky.

'My other Yiayia says the Turks take little girls, Greek girls. They steal them away and marry them.'

'Why?'

'I don't know, but Yiayia Maria says we can never to go to the Northern side. She says when you cross the border they get you. And they can have ten wives, and they're all little Greek girls, and their families never find them. Ever again.'

I feel this weight in my stomach and I think I'm going to be sick. She's probably telling me this to scare me, to make it like a sleepover. But my Daddy says never to go to the North. When Mamma asked he swore. He said 'They'll have to fucking kill me first'.

I close my eyes shut tight and count to twenty. Tomorrow we'll go back to the hotel, and me and Gali will play in the pool, and Nicky will make us laugh and we'll all eat ice cream and Mamma and Daddy will smile behind their big sunglasses.

'I don't care what they do to me,' Gali says into the silence, 'I'm never getting married.'

Chapter Thirty-Four

'How old is she?' Dex asked, candles in hand. We stood looking at the chocolate cake I'd made, *Happy Birthday Mags* in wobbly white icing on the top.

'Shut up!' I nudged him and peered around the doorframe into the living room, watching as Magda chatted away with a variety of Camden hippies, Lee attached to her side. Their smiles were honest, and most of me was so happy to see my two friends together. Except that Magda never stayed, and Lee needed to be needed. She loved the broken people the best. Maybe that was the reason for the ill feeling in my stomach, that acidic little cynic that said 'this is going to end badly'.

'Well, how many candles do we put on? Should I ask her?'

'You don't ask a woman her age!'

Dex raised an eyebrow, 'Even on her birthday, when we're here to celebrate the age she has reached?'

I rolled my eyes, and shook my head, 'You are ill-equipped to deal with this situation. Get Lee.'

'You kidding? Mags considers her a personal present, I'm not breaking that up.'

I considered him in all of this, standing still whilst everything changed. It was like going off to uni and leaving him behind again. Dexter Fabian, statue. Always there, constant. Except any girl he'd ever slept with would disagree.

'It's a bit weird, isn't it?' I started, 'them suddenly together?'

He nodded, 'Yeah, a bit. But they're so happy.'

'Yeah.' We stood quietly for a moment, just looked at them.

'Plus, I can try and convince them to make a sex tape.'

And our moment of serious conversation was over.

'Let's just put one candle on the cake, and be done with it.' I shrugged.

'No! Not one!'

'Loneliest number?'

'One means that she's so old we didn't have enough candles to reach her age!' Dex looked panicked, and I wondered if he always worried so much about people's feelings.

'When did you become a girl?'

'Hey, I have experience with women. Lots of them. All shapes, sizes and ages. In fact, you could say they're my specialist subject.'

'Yeah, Mastermind will be calling any day,' I sighed, irritated, 'so what do we do? No candles?'

His eyes lit with an idea, and he kissed me on the cheek, 'you go turn down the lights, I am on this one.'

I shrugged and did as I was told, walking into the living room and adjusting the dimmer switch. Everyone turned to look, and I swept my hands towards the kitchen, where Dex appeared holding the cake, three candles sitting in a triangle in the middle.

We sang a slow, off-key version of 'Happy Birthday', with more than a few of the guests getting Mags' name wrong. She didn't seem surprised. Lee lifted her head from Mags' shoulder and smiled. So happy, stranger girl. Finally your turn now.

She blew out the candles, we turned the lights back on. Some of the guests groaned with the sudden brightness.

'Hey Dex!' Mags called out as he returned from the kitchen, where he'd no doubt placed the cake in a precarious position on the side, and licked the icing off the bottom of the candles.

He kissed her on the cheek, 'Happy Birthday.'

'Thank you. So, why three candles?' She raised an eyebrow at me.

He shrugged like it was the most obvious thing, 'three's the magic number, babe.' Butter wouldn't melt. I was almost convinced he'd only ever had three candles on his birthday cake, every year.

Mags and Lee laughed, and I shook my head at him, 'You smooth bastard.'

'Me?' he pointed at himself, 'Golden child! Angel!' and wandered off to get another beer.

Daniel arrived and we sat together on the lumpy sofa, resting our heads back and staring at the ceiling. We'd been looking around at all the arty people, the stoners, bohemians. New age travellers, and possibly homeless. I wasn't sure I even really wanted that world. Didn't want the gallery life, didn't want the artists. What was left, except to paint and be alone?

'So, I reached a milestone of my own today,' Daniel said, grasping my hand, a dry smile in place. He sounded exhausted.

'What?'

'Today, I tattooed my fiftieth butterfly.'

I patted his hand, 'I'm so sorry.'

'There is a lack of imagination in the world, it's depressing.' He briefly pressed his face into my neck and sighed. He sat up as Lee bounced over.

'Depressing? Nope, not tonight my friend! Hello, Daniel.' She balanced on the armrest of the sofa, and kissed him on the forehead.

'Sorry, I'll perk up in a sec.'

'The world is lacking in imagination,' I explained to Lee.

'Never!'

'You don't like butterflies do you Lee?' Daniel asked.

She raised her chin to look at me, and I shook my head.

'No, no. Terrible, terrible bugs. Just bugs. Who likes bugs? Not me!'

Daniel grinned, 'not a liar by nature then?'

'Oh no, how very tiring.' She looked across the room to Mags, who winked at her and tilted her head to beckon her. Lee gave me a brief smile before moving across the room to join her.

'When did that happen?' Daniel asked, moving closer in towards me, tracing my fingertips with his own.

'Them two? Not long ago. I think it's serious though.' I sighed a little, a shuffled in irritation.

'What's the frown for?' He turned to face me, giving his full attention. Maybe that's how I'd got dragged in the first night. When Daniel listens, he focuses completely. Eye contact, body language, like he can't even register anything else. It's comforting and terrifying at the same time, like I'll never have anything interesting enough to warrant that much attention.

'Just don't want things to end. Lee deserves this, so does Mags. But they're both so...I don't know. Cynic by nature, I guess.'

He made a face, 'You, a cynic? Shocking!' He tapped out a rhythm on my thigh, and looked up to check I had got the joke, 'Well, if you feel it, it means something. I'm sure you've got a good sense of intuition.'

'Nope,' I grinned, 'it's terrible. I should absolutely do the opposite of whatever my gut instinct is.'

'I'll keep that in mind.' He kissed me, and I suddenly thought of Dex, somewhere in that room, and they hadn't even met. Sober public display of affection in a well-lit room in front of my friends? Made my stomach contract. But I liked to feel his smile against my lips.

I fidgeted and pulled back, but he just grinned and sipped his beer. Dex walked over as if I'd summoned him with my thoughts.

'Hey! Dex, have you met Daniel?' Daniel, my...what? Boyfriend? Friend? Acquaintance? Boy who knows all my secrets. Crush. Confidante. Stranger.

'Nah, nice to meet you, mate.' He swung his hand around, back to being the charmer in an instant, but gave me a look. Like he didn't know who I was anymore.

'You too,' Daniel sat up straighter, 'so you guys are old friends, right?'

'Since I was knee-high to a grasshopper!' Dex smiled, with that look of affection he turned on to fit the story he was telling. Today was apparently an Ellie's My Best Friend nostalgia trip. 'Ellie's been keeping me on the straight and narrow since she was old enough to boss anyone around.'

'Cheers for that ever so flattering personal profile. I've never managed to keep you on the straight and narrow.'

'Well, I'm definitely straight!' His laugh caught in his throat, and he beat his chest, 'I'm just gonna grab another beer, d'ya want one Dan?'

'Cheers.'

And Dex walked away.

'So, that's your best friend.'

'Childhood best friend. He's tying for first place with Lee. Lee's less work.'

He looked at me for a moment, and brushed a strand of hair out of my eye, stroking my cheek.

'I really like you, you know.'

'Me too...'

'...but?'

'No but. Just a pause.' I snapped, irritated that once again I never knew what to say or how to say it.

Daniel slouched back into the sofa, out of my personal space and smiled at the ceiling.

'All I mean is, when the time comes where you freak out and push me away, I'm not going to let you fuck this up. Okay?'

I snickered, and leaned my head on his shoulder, 'deal.'

I watched Lee and Magda across the room, smiling, happy, together. And I linked my hand with Daniel, and thought maybe it was okay, maybe we were all moving on, and it would be completely fine, natural.

I saw Dex standing in the kitchen, a beer in each hand, wearing his charming grin and his heart in his boxers, but, for once, there was no-one there to fall for it.

Chapter Thirty-Five

His name's Jack, and I've given him half my drugs and all my heart by eleven pm. He's beautiful. Not just in his eyes and skin and body, but in his thoughts and dreams and wonderings about the world. He thinks about things that I can't imagine, twisting words around like pipe cleaners, until I feel like one of those little mice in the plastic tunnels.

I think it's that he's not talking about himself, he's offering up thoughts on platters, afraid of what his guests will think, how they will digest, but still sure that he's giving the best he has.

His eyes are a muddy blue, and I think he's wearing eyeliner.

He takes my hand before we're introduced, and says only 'We're the same.'

I say 'yes!' and we go to dance. I think I love him.

I know, I know in my head full of pain and drugs and joy that this is just chemical. A change in hormones, fixed in time with the pounding of the bass and the delirious deliciousness of shaking and jumping and dancing. But I love him. In thirty seconds of dancing, hands clasped, heads banging, shoulders touching, I wander city streets, go on holidays, stay in, get married, have kids, and die holding hands with this man. He is a soul above and beyond me, and this will be the start of my story, my movie moment. This will be my O'Hara kiss, my Roman princess escape. He will be my Cary Grant, and I'll be quick and excellent and witty, forever and ever.

There is no Dex here tonight. He's at home with a cold, his Dad fussing over him, and I'll admit, part of me wanted to stay there and look after him, but most of me loves that he's not here to see this. I don't even want to prove anything, I don't have to compete. I just met an important person and it was all fate and consequence.

'Shall we take it higher?' He grabs my hand and leads me to the disabled toilets, where we slip inside. He holds out my bare arm, and snorts a line from it, the little hairs standing up. After, he licks from the inside of my wrist down in one wiggle, getting the last traces. 'Your turn'. I do the same.

I feel the odd desire to keep him in that dingy toilet in the club, to let him shag me. Not even let him, but make a move, make him want me, show him that it's alright. That I don't care where or when, just that it's him and it's fine and wonderful.

We dance for what seems like no time, until he says we should go back to his, and even Lee sees that my bouncing way is not like all the other times, when she asks the address and tells me to be safe. He holds my hand on the bus, and mutters into my hair, stroking softly, and tells me about the first time he remembers hurting, (scraping his knee on a swing) and the possibility of wormholes ('we only know a tiny fraction of what is possible. We don't know the impossible, Ellie, how can we?') until I am sleepy and satisfied and humming with anticipation.

We reach his warm house, and he makes tea. We sit and talk and I find I'm not even hearing the words, just admiring the chocolate drip of his voice as if slithers across the sofa, silkens my skin and wraps around me like a blanket. I love you, I love you, I love you. Don't stay a stranger, tell me everything, tell me more of you, everything I can take. I want you, you.

I watch as his pouty mouth outlines sounds, and feel the softness inside his wrist as he smiles at me.

'Bed?' the sun is coming up, and he wraps his arms around me. His bed is soft and enveloping, and he wraps his arms around me, his lips against my neck. This is it, this is right. I count to two hundred before I roll over, ignoring his sleep, and kiss him. He stirs, so I try again. His eyes open.

'No Ellie, that's not what this is. It's just the high, that's all.' He still keeps an arm round me, but it's looser, further away, and my body is cold. I roll back over and pretend to yawn, 'Of course, sure.' I say, trying to seem carefree, drug-addled, a confusion in etiquette. Sleep-kissing, that's what it was. I woke up in a stranger's bed, and thought he was my lover, because I do this so often.

I lay awake for three hours, replaying those ten seconds when everything fell apart, and when I finally agree I can stop looking at him and leave, I creep out, jump on the bus, then the tube, and go home.

I walk in around ten am and say nothing. I wipe off my make up, change into my pyjamas and stare at myself in my bedroom mirror, willing myself to cry. All I want to do is cry. Cry it out, the night, the salty drug tears, the hormones and the mistakes and the stupidity. Don't confuse chemical and real, don't make fun into feelings. Don't make one night friends into one night stands.

I can't cry. Instead, I crawl into bed, pull the cover over my head, and pretend to be sick. I tell my mum I have what Dex has, and she makes me chicken soup, strokes my hair, and tells me everything will be alright. I have no choice but to believe her. And in the morning, Jack is not a beautiful boy, or a possibility, or even a prophet. He is a person, who in the light of day, is no doubt nowhere near as interesting, and I try to deal with the fact that he is probably thinking the same about me.

Chapter Thirty-Six

It was a quiet night at home, after a day out at the student protests. The country was going crazy suddenly, and us jobless graduates and future students were in the middle of it. Fighting for it. Politics was relevant all of a sudden, and it scared me how much everything could change. Another rise in university fees, and would all these young graduates in debt be just like me and my friends, jobless and back home again? We sang songs in Leicester Square, but the atmosphere got too charged, and me and Lee left. That evening on the news we watched as it escalated into chaos, saw them smashing shop fronts on Oxford Street. Somehow being part of a movement didn't seem as important when the children on the television couldn't even explain what they were fighting for. I felt old.

But it made me want to do something again, stop lulling about. It made me want to paint, and I had the house to myself. Nicky was still holed up in his room, refusing to leave the house. Dad was out, and I didn't want to think where. Mum was having a much deserved night out.

So I set up my canvas, my easel, all the little parts of my ritual. I'd missed it. I had nothing to paint, so I was playing. It was as good as it could be, whilst I was still jobless. At least I was doing something.

Then my mobile rang. Dex. I was just too serene for anyone else, though. He'd want me to go out, go drinking, or go to his or give my opinion on a girl. Or else, he'd just want me to hang out with him and be his Ellie. I was too tired to be anyone's anything. I just wanted to be alone, not trying, not defined, not even an 'I'. Just a person who was painting. That was fine. The phone finally stopped. Then he tried again. I wavered slightly, but carried on swirling my brush in the blue paint, a perfect sapphire, colour of silk. Don't pick up. Don't pick up. Don't want to talk or go or be. Just want to paint.

I stuck the phone under my pillow, and returned to the canvas, a series of faint grey pencil scratches, the barest guidelines. Just shaded enough to not be a terrifying blank space, awaiting ruin, but not so planned that I couldn't be spontaneous. Finally created the conditions for Making Art. Finally. It had been months.

Then the house phone rang. Let the machine get it, don't move, you've achieved something wonderful here, Ellie, don't do it. Don't become, not yet. It's fine, the outside world doesn't need you. House phone stopped. And then started again.

And then I heard his voice.

'Ellie! Let me in!'

Dex was outside my house. Dex was shouting, probably drunk, outside my front door. I put down my brush, stroked the dry canvas. Not this time. And whatever I was going to do now wouldn't happen. I wouldn't feel like it tomorrow. Whatever I felt after Dex had finally fucked off would not be what I felt like painting before he arrived. Ruined. Lost in time.

I marched downstairs, ready to give the intrusive bastard a piece of my mind.

But when I saw him, nodding away to non-existent music on my doorstep, I realised he wasn't drunk. I looked at his pupils, huge and black, almost banishing his irises. He was fucked.

'What did you take?' I ushered him into the house, thankful that my dad wasn't home.

'What you ALWAYS take!' He laughed.

I pulled him into the kitchen and pushed him into a chair. Then I ran the tap and handed him a glass of water. He looked at me in childlike delight, like I'd read his mind. He downed the glass in one, dribbling down his chin. The water splotched his damp green t-shirt, already soaked through with sweat.

'Since when do you do drugs? You don't take drugs.' I sat down opposite him, suddenly feeling like a parent, disappointed. Expecting so much more of someone who was clearly incapable.

'But you do! And you feel happy!' He grinned sloppily, and drummed out an uneven rhythm on the kitchen table, tracing the scratches in the wood.

'It's not real, it's just chemical.'

'Nah, Ellie, darling, you're always having a good time! The best time, the best time anyone ever has! But you're cool, yeah, you're cool, super cool, so you've got to pretend it's not a big deal. You're not lonely or anything, you're just super cool, with your drugs, and those boys you never let fuck you.'

I sat back in the chair and just looked at him. His dark hair more bedraggled than usual, shining with sweat and those awkward hands that he couldn't keep still. The shivering would start soon enough. He nodded his head up and down as his jaw started chewing. He looked surprised, and I went to search through my coat pockets for some gum so he wouldn't grind away at his teeth.

I threw the pack a little more violently than necessary.

'Hey!'

'Why did you do this?'

'I wanna be like you-oo-ou!' He sang, throwing his head back, and I grabbed his chin tightly.

'Dexter, look at me. Why did you do this?'

'I wanted to feel happy! And it made you happy, and I thought we could be happy together! But you're not on this, and I don't like it. Why don't I feel happy?' His voice seemed separate from his body, like he was looking in on himself. Which he probably was.

I sighed and stroked his hair gently.

'I don't feel so good.'

His body was exalted, and his mind was terrified. He was stuck in between the chemical and the emotional. Why, why did he do it? Stupid, stupid fucker. It could have been brilliant, the first time Dex did ecstasy. We could have been together, I could have guided him, taught him. The way he'd taught me all those other things years ago. He would have been himself, but just so much happier. Except that he wouldn't have been himself. Because Dex didn't do drugs.

'I've missed you. And I thought I would do this. Because you do this. And you used to do it by yourself. And now you can do it with him.'

'Him?'

'Daniel.'

'Yes, Daniel does it too. But I haven't been doing it as much.' If it was any other time, I could have told him about Yiayia. Explained myself, in one of the few times when Dex was being serious. Except that either he'd get even more upset, the chemicals screwing with him, or he'd feel overly empathetic, unable to understand how I was holding myself together. Or he wouldn't feel anything, and would panic.

'I noticed. It's because of him?' He paused, 'Daniel.'

'In some ways.'

'You're happy,' he said.

I shrugged.

'I'm not happy,' he said simply.

'Really?'

'Not without the booze and the bravado, and the girls.'

'Then carry on with that, carry on being happy. You're in your twenties, there's nothing wrong with having fun.' I whispered to him, trying so hard to be for him the person Lee was for me. Give him guidance without judgement, see exactly what he wanted from me.

'But now you're happy without your drugs, and now Daniel...' he whispered back.

I just looked at him, exasperated. 'I don't understand.'

'You're happy without them, and I'm ready to be happy without them.'

'So, that's good, right?'

I went to fetch him another glass of water until he caught hold of me, whimpering like I'd abandoned him.

'I thought you were waiting for me...' His eyes were unfocused, and I felt like I could have been anyone. He could have been rattling away his thoughts to anyone. Except that he was Dex, and I was Ellie, and I'd completely missed the point.

Deep breath, flounder, think. The words *you just don't want me to be happy,* formed in my head, followed by *I don't love you, I was never enough for you, I never will be.* I stamped them down, horrified.

'Sweetie, things change, by themselves, I didn't do anything...it just happened.'

'I know,' he said, pouting like a child, tears in his eyes, 'Lee and Mags getting together. You quitting that stupid gallery job, and meeting Daniel and not doing *this* anymore. Everyone's moving on. And I'm still in that fucking cafe.'

'Then quit! You don't need me for that! Quit Baby's and quit the girls and the booze and the shagging. Start fresh.'

He scowled at me, 'Oh it's all so easy now, is it Ellie? Now you don't need strangers on drugs to tell you they love you.'

I wanted to tell him Yiayia had died, to shock him into terror and guilt. I wanted him rocking back and forth in the corner of the room. I couldn't even find the energy to slap him, though I wanted to. I suddenly wanted to hurt him more than anyone in the world.

'What, so now you're ready? Want me waiting in the wings for when you've finished fucking everything that moves? What's the matter, Dex, run out of girls to shag in London?'

'You said you wanted to be friends!' He shouted.

'And I did! I do! I am!'

I pushed back from the table, and stood over him, 'I have been nothing but supportive. You pushed me away once, and I came back. You've never fought for me. You've just decided to get your life together, and I'm a safe bet, someone to tell you what to do.'

'That's not...' he whined, and squinted up at me.

'What do you want from me, Dex?'

'What do you fucking think!'

'I don't know! I've never fucking known!' I screamed back at him.

Nicky was suddenly standing in the doorway, a large shadow, strong form. He frowned at Dex, as if he hadn't known him since he was a kid. As if he didn't like him very much at all.

'Dexter, I think it's time to go, mate.'

Dex looked up in pure shock at Nicky, Nicky who was his friend, who had always joked with him and been kind. Nicky nodded. Dex stumbled to his feet, and we followed him to the front door.

He turned to face me, 'I'm...I just miss you. I thought...I don't know, I'm all fucked. I don't like this.'

I took his hand, 'Look, you go home, and you wrap up in your comfiest duvet, and watch your favourite comedy on TV. Drink water, but not too much. Just think about all the things you love.' I gave my instructions with authority, the doctor is in session. *Take two of these and call me in the morning.*

I thought he was going to ask to stay, but he nodded, suddenly shy and ashamed.

Dex mumbled an apologetic goodbye to Nicky, looked at me searchingly whilst I didn't meet his eyes, and closed the door behind him. I leaned against the door, worn down like I'd fought a hundred rounds and still hadn't won.

'Saw that coming,' Nicky snorted.

'No you didn't.' I didn't feel like painting at all. I just felt like curling up in a ball, and ignoring the world. My nose tingled, and when I touched my cheeks they were wet. My throat closed up and I felt my shoulders shake.

'Want to see if there's any ridiculous shit on TV?' Nicky offered, putting an arm around me. There were dark circles under his eyes, his skin was pale. His tatty, worn clothes were loose. He looked like the Nicky I'd lost all those years ago. Except he was here, holding onto me.

'I love you,' I said shakily.

'Weirdo,' he replied.

Nicky squeezed me briefly and went to switch on the kettle. We spent a strange evening mocking terrible television shows, and drinking more tea than I thought possible. We didn't really laugh, but we were a distraction for each other.

When I went up to bed, my hands grazed the canvas sitting by my window, where the shapes I'd drawn suddenly looked unrecognisable.

Chapter Thirty-Seven

'So that was it?' I ask, smiling to myself as I pull my hoodie back over my head. Nirvana. The cross-eyed smiley face is flaking off the front, and I tell myself that's all I can expect from Camden market. Should have bought it from the seller down by the Thai place, instead of the 'two for twenty' guy. It's two sizes too big and always smells slightly damp. But it makes me feel safe, telling everyone what I like and who I am.

'Hey, I'll have you know I gave it my very best effort.' Dex grins at me, his brown, fluffy hair standing up on end as he pulls his leg through his inside-out jeans, crumpled on the floor.

'I'm very sorry, I appreciate your services, truly.'

'Services? I took no payment, it was a favour for a friend.'

I roll my eyes as I slide my jeans back up, 'Way to make a girl feel attractive Dex, cheers for that.'

'Hey, I had a good time.' He smiles in that way he used to when we were kids, like you're the only thing he sees, like you're special. 'Really.'

'Well, now that's sorted, I guess I better get back to that important stuff, like GCSEs and figuring out a career. All that crap.' I start for the door, where my bag is waiting, ready to get out as quickly as possible. I knew this was going to happen. I anticipated the awkwardness.

Dex pulls a t-shirt over his head, and I only then notice how scrawny he is, how much of his attractiveness comes from his charm and confidence, not his body. It hadn't felt great. It hadn't felt anything like I imagined it would, but then, Dex doesn't love me. He's just a boy who has experience, who loves to love, as he likes to say. And yes, I love him, a little. I spent all that time thinking about the kisses and the strokes, the kind words and the moment, that one moment, when we'd be connected. I didn't think about the state of his mismatched sheets, or that his dad was next door sleeping, or even what I was meant to feel. I feel sore, and empty and relieved. This is what everyone's talking about? No big deal.

I distinctly remember being kissed, my first kiss, and being bitterly disappointed. Not even disappointed. Disgusted. I moaned, and moped and blamed Disney for lying to me. I asked Dex how he could bear to have sex when kissing was so disgusting. He just grinned and told me I was doing it wrong.

And now he's looking at me like I've done something wrong again.

'What?'

'You, you don't have to go now, you know,' he smiles, 'we could watch something? I could make tea.'

Somehow, to Dex, making tea is a big deal. I imagine he rarely makes anything for the conquests he brings home. I'm about to run, about to leave him to be that person he is, and go back to my life, where I've made friends with a girl called Lee, who feels like me, who sits on the edge of that group of beautiful people at school. We get each other, and Dex just slides through those girls like they're on a conveyor belt, not caring that they're all the same. And I suppose that I am one of those girls now. It doesn't really upset me.

'Yeah,' I drop the bag on the floor, 'that'd be nice.'

So he brings up tea and toast on a little tray, and he's remembered that when we were kids I used to put a slice of cheese on top of my marmalade, and puts a piece on the side of the plate. He remembers that I drink my tea extra strong, two sugars. And we sit and watch a ridiculous amount of Buffy the Vampire Slayer on VHS. Later on we share a joint, and when I get up to leave, he buries his face in my neck.

'I'm really glad we're friends again, Ellie.'

His warmth is comforting, and he smells like him, and I have missed him, the bastard. Even though it is his fault we weren't friends, because he's beautiful and popular, and can't bear to even talk about what happened with his mum. Because I tried to push him to talk to me about it one day, and he told me to fuck off. And I did. So I guess we're both to blame.

'We're not going to be friends who do this though Dex, are we?' I don't let it sound like a question, more a warning, gesturing between the two of us.

'No, no! Strictly a one time deal. Grass is greener, you know me!' He puffs up his chest and winks, and I think suddenly that he's not beautiful, he's just a nice guy. A massive goofball, an old friend. An endless possibility. I've missed him, and we'll try again, this friendship thing.

'But El, we can do this again, right, the TV and the tea and stuff? Just, hang around, I mean.' He throws an arm around my shoulder, and I can't help but smile. Dexter Fabiano wants to be my friend! If only the girls at school knew that, I'd be the Queen Bee.

But I don't want to be Queen of anything. I don't want to do anything except get through the day without worrying about boys and sex and where my life's going and what my dad's said now.

Dex doesn't exactly make me feel beautiful, but he makes me feel like I'm something else, something wanted. Someone he's missed. And so I kiss him on the cheek, and tell him to come meet my friend Lee, we'll go somewhere. Yes, he's my friend again, and no, he can't fuck her.

There's not enough moments in life where you can sit there, having conquered something you were scared of, and think 'Well, that wasn't important at all, that was nothing.'

Lost my virginity and got my old friend back. A perfect transaction.

Chapter Thirty-Eight

'Hey,' I said into the sunlight. The cemetery was beautiful, grass strangely green, like I'd wandered into a place that was trying too hard. Stepford. Hiding something terrible behind something beautiful. Except that the terrible was the beautiful. The silence, the link between every living person in there, who had experienced loss, who had felt that gut wrenching pain, that betrayal. Every loss is an abandonment, whether you choose it or not.

'So, apparently you're still here,' I mouthed to the shabby cross sitting in the upturned earth, offensive in its simplicity. Everyone kept telling me it wasn't permanent, we were just waiting for the big marble monstrosity my dad would have made in honour of his mother. I didn't know which was worse. 'Apparently, according to the church, and all our family members, you're hanging around until the forty days is up. You're just checking everything out, right? Making sure we're all good? Then, next week, you get to float off into the light, and sit on fluffy clouds, right?'

The cemetery had no place to sit, and unlike all those films I'd seen where people converse with their deceased friends into the evening, I hovered awkwardly.

This was so stupid. What did I think was going to happen? A tree would shake in the wind and I'd know she was there; I'd feel comforted, I'd suddenly understand? Dad wouldn't go to the cemetery because it was still too raw, and no-one else went because you just don't do that. You wait and you suffer through forty days, where you don't laugh, and you cry and you wear black. And then you go back for mimosino, where you get tricked into going to Sunday Service at the church. You stand about for hours in that cold drafty building with the gilded gold ceilings, where they go on and on in that language that isn't mine, and at the end they read out her name, which is my name, so I die along with her.

Then we stop wearing black, and we stop remembering. And everything's fine.

'What you did, Yiayia, what you did...' I couldn't even say it in my own head, or to a piece of wood tilted in the earth.

'You should have listened to the doctors. You could have been happy again, they would have, it's such a...waste. All because you had to be in control, couldn't wait. You're so good at keeping secrets, aren't you?' I took a deep breath, 'I'm like that, I'm so scared that I'm like you. And now you've given me one more secret to keep, haven't you? Thanks for that. Just what I needed.'

I imagined her sad face, tilting with a lack of understanding. A small twitch of the lips to let me know she loved me anyway. Watery blue eyes that saw exactly who I was, who patted my hand and apologised. Maybe her face would darken, or she'd raise an eyebrow and say what was Nicky's favourite phrase as a child: *filas din mana sou magina de stoma*? She'd know, just from my expression, my tone. *Do you talk to your mother with that mouth?*

I couldn't carry on talking to a piece of wood, or the dead earth that sat upon her dead body. I pictured her, beneath layers of earth, already fading, decomposing. I thought of all those biology classes, where they tell you that a corpse's fingernails keep growing, and their hair keeps growing, and I just had this image of a dead man, his fingernails scratching out of his own coffin, year by year, poking into the one next to his, like a tree that refuses to die. Infecting everything.

I thought of all those history classes, where they tell you about how the Egyptian's mummified their corpses, the different serums they used, how they took out the brains, because what use were they? And in China, they can't dress the corpse in red clothes, because that means happiness, and what corpse is happy? It turns them into a ghost and they are forced to stay on earth.

Perhaps we should have dressed you in red, Yiayia, to keep you with us. Perhaps we should have kept you on the valium, in your red dresses, with your strained smiles and your tired eyes. How would you have known what happiness was? How would you have known the difference? Everything's fuzzy and fine, and okay. Just okay, never more. And that's good enough for most people, why not for you? Knowing is the worst. Knowing things that would kill other people, and so you hold onto them, keep it burning inside so it doesn't seep out beyond you. It stops with me, stops with Nicky.

How much did you know, Yiayia? If Dad knew what I know about you, it would kill him. And what did you know about Dad? Did you know what he's been doing, did you guess? Do you know now? Do you know anything beyond cold earth and growing fingernails and a silk-lined coffin? What if you did know, if you knew everything, the way I always thought when I was a kid, that you were magical, beyond us, understanding not only a different language, but a different world. If you knew all those horrible things about the way people really are, and did nothing, are you even the person I thought?

I was the only person who could hide anything from you, and I never did.

It was pointless, and I don't know what I hoped to achieve. Maybe that if I stood near her body, whatever part of her existed in the ether would hear what I was thinking, know what was going on. I didn't expect an answer.

I kept her secret with Nicky, I kept Dad's secret on my own. And after enough time, it becomes easy to forget the truth, because you can talk about the lie with such sincerity. Make it a good story, one with a moral, with a rhythm, a point. Hell, make it a limerick, and give it a happy ending.

'I'm so fucking tired,' I sighed, letting my eyes rest once more on the embarrassing little stick in the ground, nowhere near enough for her. It would be replaced after the church service, the end of the forty days. The end of my penitence, when life went back to how it was before. Then there'd be that big marbled plaque competing with the other Greek graves surrounding it. Somber and magnificent and completely without personality. But how do you make a lump of marble represent a human? It's cold, and unmoving, and eternal.

I had to walk through a field of graves to get back to my car, the black ants of another funeral parade. And like a typical Londoner, my feelings of empathy for these strangers who had lost someone faded abruptly as I realised they had locked me in to these tiny fake roads throughout this strange dead village. I couldn't move for the cars of the people who loved a dead man. I sat in the car for half an hour, watching as more and more people said goodbye to this stranger. Little Greek women wobbling around as they climbed up hills to gravesides, young boys in too-big suits, and little girls in uncomfortable shoes. Every girl looked like me and Gali, every Aunt and Uncle like copies of my own. Dark and sombre and completely proper. The priest started his explanations, the swift moves of his hands through the air. No-one broke into dramatic sobs, and I watched as

194

the silver pendulum swung, releasing incense in wafts that would always smell like church, and loss.

The singing of the priest lulled me to sleep, and when I woke they were gone.

Chapter Thirty-Nine

'Hello, Ellie, sweetheart,' Dex's dad patted my arm as he ushered me into the house. Tim always moved slowly, like he was recovering from a fight. He had a gentle voice, and kind eyes and looked absolutely nothing like Dex, except when they quirked their eyebrows in confusion or disbelief.

'Had the night shift?'

'Yeah, last few weeks now, it's killing me love, I'm telling you,' he clicked the kettle on, and I sat at the breakfast bar, as I must have a hundred times before, wiggling onto the bar stool and tapping my nails on the blue tiled top. Dex's house always made me feel like a kid again.

'You won't say no to a cuppa, surely?'

'Have I ever said no?' I smiled, 'his royal highness up yet?'

Tim put my tea in front of me, just the way I liked it, and sat opposite, a packet of biscuits between us.

'The only reason I knew he was in the house was because I fell over his shoes on the way in this morning,' he dunked the biscuit in his tea, 'that boy has stupidly big feet.'

I smirked, and we forgot about waiting for Dex as we talked about everything else. He asked me how my job was, and what my plans were, and listened to everything I said. He told me I'd have no problem, that I was a talented and anyone could see that. He said that it wouldn't last forever, I just had to get through this slump. That soon enough everything would set itself right. The comforting Dad-like things to say.

I suppose, thinking about it, Dex had his charm, his easy manner, being happy to chat away, but Tim was softer, more domesticated. He knew how to look after people, he'd had to learn quickly. He had the demeanor of a man who knew what it felt like to not be enough for someone. To wake up one morning and find everything was different. He was careful to make sure no-one else felt like that.

Tim worked at the hospital, and we chatted about the different terrible things that happened, and sometimes, the amazing instances in which people survived. It gave me a sense of perspective that lasted all of half an hour.

'You don't have to stay up and keep me company,' I patted his hand, 'you must be knackered. I've got a book, I know where the kettle is. If he's not up in half an hour, I'll throw a bucket of water over him.'

Tim looked at me with such frank affection that I was suddenly embarrassed.

'You're a good girl, Ellie,' he held my hand, and squeezed, 'when my shit-for-brains son is going to wake up and see that, I don't know.'

He was putting away the biscuits when Dex finally appeared. A girl in last night's clubbing clothes followed him. She didn't have the good sense to look abashed.

'Afternoon, sunshine!' I saluted him with my mug, 'Good night?'

'Not bad,' he yawned, trying to look relaxed. 'Did you...er, want some coffee or anything?' He directed the question to the girl, and Tim tutted loudly. It was obvious Dex couldn't remember her name. That's why I always got out early. Why give anyone a chance to pretend?

'Who's she?' Conquered Conquest asked Dex, jutting her chin towards me. I waved, over-friendly, completely at ease. *This is my domain, darling. You are merely passing through.*

'My friend.'

'Girlfriend?'

'No, just a *friend*,' I replied for him, smiling sweetly. He always picks the stupid ones. It's not like there weren't pretty, *smart* drunk girls willing to go home with him, but always with the shit-for-brains. Maybe it made him feel less guilty. Or more superior.

'Oh.'

'Do you want me to walk you to the tube station?' he looked at her pointedly.

'Nah, see you around. I had fun.' She kissed him on the mouth, slippery sounds abound, and then exited. Her hair was dyed blackest black, and her panda eyes actually looked quite appealing. As she turned, her short skirt swung, and I found her more endearing when I noticed how her thighs wobbled when she walked.

He followed her to the front door, and there was silence as he closed it. I watched Tim, staring down at the sink, scrubbing at the washing up forcefully.

'Any tea for me, Dad?' Dex smiled as he appeared again. The Angel Child. Tim just looked up at him and shook his head, patted my arm as he walked by, and trudged up to bed.

Dex's smile faded briefly, then clicked back into place.

'I swear, they're never that stupid the night before,' he started on the biscuits, spilling crumbs everywhere. Big hands, clumsy. Trying to hide the hangover. Or he was so accustomed to it, he didn't even notice it anymore.

'You don't talk to them the night before.'

'I chat them up,' he points out, slipping into Tim's surrendered seat. 'That involves talking to them.' He dunked a biscuit into my tea, and I glared.

'That involves talking *at* them, and seeing which one of them falls for it. Then you spend the rest of the time sticking your tongue down their throat.' I laughed. 'Fill the kettle, would you Casanova?'

He did so, and asked from under those Bambi lashes, 'You're not angry at me, are you?'

'Darling, please. When have I ever been angry at you for being you?'

Occasionally, when I was lonely, and I'd just left the house of a boy who'd been my confidante, my dearest friend, a symbol of everything that was good, for eighteen hours or so, I thought of Dex. In my moments of solitude, on a comedown, I pictured him doing all those things with different girls, things that seemed off-putting, awkward out of context, but I imagined made sense when you wanted someone completely. Loved them, maybe. I'd never really desired anyone, and Dex had been the first to claim there was something very wrong with me.

'That sounds like you're having a go.'

'It sounds like morning-after remorse, on your part.'

'You've always judged me.' His voice rose, indignant.

'And you've always been like this. I've never expected anything else from you. I'm your friend, not your conscience. You wanna feel guilty, fine. But it's not *me* making you feel guilty!'

'Yes it is!' Dex shouted at me, and a stamping came from the ceiling. Tim, telling us to keep it down, so he could sleep.

We sat in silence as he poured the hot water into the mugs, let the teabags steep. Put exactly the right amount of milk in. Stirred three times clockwise and once anti-clockwise. The same way since forever.

'When was the last time you had sex when you were sober?' I asked. He looked at me, and didn't say anything, and I didn't want it to be true. I shook my head.

'When was the last time you had sex?' He asked softly, and that time, I was the one to stare, too ashamed to say the words.

We spent the rest of the day on the sofa, watching shitty movies and not saying much, careful not to lean against each other, or touch at all. In the afternoon we would meet Mags and Lee at the pub, and it would start all over again. I was still wearing black.

Chapter Forty

He's possibly the most beautiful boy I've ever seen, and I'm young and nervous and drinking too much. We're at a bar in Clapham that is one part pretentious, three parts awesome. But I feel unattractive and so stupidly coltish in my polka dot dress and oversized glasses. I'm more suited for a tea dance than a night club, and apparently that's the plan.

It's three months till uni, and I'm counting down the days. These are Dexter's friends, and when I say 'friends', I mean 'people he stumbled into on a night out and has charmed along with us'. Damien is the beautiful boy's name, and I can't stare at him directly. He's the first one who looks like Dex.

'Slow down, darling, or the night will be over before you know it!' He slings an arm around me in that comforting way some people have, glowing. He's never had to deal with someone not liking him, or maybe he doesn't care. His eyes are light and hair is dark, and he's wearing these black braces with shiny buckles attached to his jeans. He should look ridiculous, but he doesn't.

'Besides, drinking's a waste compared with everything else there is,' he pulls me closer, and I'm forced to actually look at him head-on. I feel Dex's wary eyes, and smile at him, jutting out my chin.

'Like what?'

Damien's grin is electric, and he starts to move, jerky excited movements. He reminds me of a puppy, 'Like the feeling that you've found a soulmate, who will love you and never judge you and get you, just get exactly what you mean. That you can feel not alone. Truly with someone else for six to eight hours, and everything is beautiful.'

He strokes my fingertips and doesn't look at me, 'What do you think?'

'It sounds beautiful,' I admit.

'You think you want to play my game, little one?' He draws closer, tracing a thumb across my lower lip.

'Only if you stop being a patronising arse about it all,' I raise an eyebrow, and he laughs loudly, kissing me on the temple.

'I like you!'

'I like you too,' I'm confident now, sure that I'm in with the cool kids, that I'm finally about to have an adventure beyond weed and bacardi breezers and whatever drama Dex has created that week. 'So, where's the magic pill that will make me amazing?'

He crooks a finger, 'Shall we disappear to the garden for a bit?'

I jump down on the excitement that rises up, because he's not asking because he fancies me, but because he wants to share something he thinks is important. Damien will continue to be an accidental pusher, an enlightener, whichever term fits best. He's lead many a new traveller down the path to ecstasy, and has never once dealt or had too much. A true believer in the religion of feeling connected.

So we disappear to the back corner of a garden, where he explains that 'usually, I'd just tell you to go to the bathroom and snort it, but I figure you're not so experienced...'

'In this, anyway,' I grin, because why not be a flirt when adventure is abound?

'Oh, I'm sure you're terribly talented in other ways, darling,' his posh voice is tinged with that cockney affectation, and I stroke a piece of hair back from his face, so that he grins at me. 'You're going to love this, honestly, I can tell. You, you're going to get it. Not everyone does.'

He hands me a screwed up piece of rizla, 'Swallow, like a pill.' I wash it down with the water he gives me. It tastes like wet paper, and very little else.

He dips his hand into his pocket again, and his fingertip emerges dusted in a yellowish-white. He rubs it into his gums delicately, and makes a face, 'a little extra for luck.'

He tilts his head to the side and leans closer, 'want to share?'

I shrug, raise an eyebrow, and he kisses me. He's warm and funny, and tastes salty, that sharp acidic taste in his mouth suddenly in mine, but I don't care because he's beautiful and he likes me.

We spend the rest of the night huddled on that bench, chatting shit, complete and utter nonsense. He delights in my delight, and together we laugh and cuddle and hold hands and tilt our heads back to look at the stars until our necks hurt. Then, we run in and dance, though the music's no good, and we try to explain to our friends that they're wonderful, beautiful humans, but they don't get it. They just laugh at us, call us pillheads.

Dexter's disappointed face flashes in front of me for longer than I want it to, and he starts questioning me until I start to feel that familiar stomach-clamping sensation that I carry around with me all the time. Shame.

'Seriously, why on earth would you do this? What's wrong with you?' His arm is around another girl, and his hand is in hair, the same way that Damien's arm is around my waist. I can only stare at him in incomprehension.

'Why would you want to make me sad right now?' I ask in awe, 'Can't you see how happy I am? Why wouldn't you want me to be happy?'

'Because it's not real,' Dexter rolls his eyes, and drags the girl off to a dark corner. She glares at me from behind panda eyes and fake eyelashes.

Damien squeezes my hand, 'Don't worry about it, darling Ellie, don't worry! You just can't let other people pull down your buzz.' He drags me out to the garden again, and we sit on that same bench, and I start to feel everything slipping away again, until I'm just some sad fraud, sitting on a bench with a boy who's too pretty for her.

'Ellie, look at me,' his eyes are serious and darker than before, 'it's like when you drink. Your emotions define your night out, right? When you drink and you're sad, you get morose. When you drink and you're happy, you get cheerful.' He put a hand on my cheek, 'don't let anyone else tear it away from you. Focus on how you feel. Focus on what makes you happy.'

I look at him, pretty boy who likes all the things I like, and is confident and happy and thinks that I'm special and beautiful, and I believe him. So I kiss him for a while longer, and then we go back to his, where we sit and talk until our throats hurt. We cuddle up on the sofa of his student house, and trace shapes on each other's arms, relishing the contact. We watch stupid movies and smokd joints and laugh and feel and connect, like I can't remember having connected with anyone.

And in the morning, when I wake up, his heavy arm around me, and I feel disconnected from everything, all I can think is 'Everyone's alone'. Sure, Damien wakes up, and offers me tea, and explains that I feel this way because of the lack of seratonin, that I will probably be without an appetite for a while, and that a joint might help. We finish the movie from the night before, but he isn't that same boy from last night. He is as alone as I am, suddenly a stranger, stuck in his own head. He isn't as beautiful as I had thought, nor as connected or intelligent or...anything. He's a nice guy, and I still see him about. I'm glad it was him.

On the bus ride home in the morning, I make a list of all the things I wish I had that would make me feel okay: facewipes, a toothbrush, gum, a comfy hoodie, a scarf, some clean socks. And I jump off at Camden market to buy myself a purple bag. Because I am going to do it again. And it is only going to get better.

Chapter Forty-One

Nicky hadn't left the house in weeks. He stayed locked inside that tiny box room of his most of the time. As far as we could see, the windows were open, the light was coming in. He ventured down to the kitchen when he thought he could avoid conversation with people. My father called him a selfish bastard. My mother said he was a sensitive boy.

Neither mentioned their real worries, about what Nicky was going to do now, no-one to care for, no-one to rely on him. Looking after Yiayia had given him purpose. Made him feel worthy, useful. Neither of them mentioned the drugs, or that dreaded word- Manchester.

After trying to get him to come out, or even just sit in and talk with him, I'd given up. There had to be an easier way, but if he wanted to be alone, he deserved to have that. He had no visitors, he didn't go out. No way to find drugs. I don't think our parents realised that was the point.

For my parents, when their kids have fucked up (if they've fucked up badly enough) it is legitimate to never mention it again. Pretend the whole embarrassing incident was just a dream. They used to refer to the drugs as 'Nicky's issues' like it wasn't a chemical imbalance but a mental one. My parents still lived in an age where having a joint was a big deal, and only rock stars took heroin.

But Mum had reached the end of the line. She had made her decision to get on with her life, and everyone else should do the same. She brought up a sandwich, carefully cut into triangles (no crusts) and a cup of tea on a little tray, a plate with two chocolate digestives on the side.

Peace offering. Wheedle her way in with food and caffeine, then go in for the kill. She nodded to me as she went in, like I was her accomplice, like she was saying 'If I'm not back in half an hour, send reinforcements'. She was scared, and desperate, stretching up on her toes like a ballerina scared to balance.

She shut the door, and I stood in the hallway to listen in.

'Nicky, I think it's time to come out of your room now.'

'Mum, I can't, not-'

'Nicholas, it is a *beautiful* day out there, and it's about time you got back in the world.'

Quiet, as he contemplated her strategy, understood that she loved him, but knew she wouldn't listen.

'Nina-' he started.

'I am your *Mother*, Nicholas, and I am in charge of looking after you. And I need you to be an adult about this-'

'What the fuck do you think I'm doing all this for? Do you think I want to be in here, locked away? I'm nearing the end of my twenties, Mum, and what do I have to show? Nothing! I want to be out there, but it's too fucking dangerous for me!'

'Nikos-'

'*Then ego dipota!*' He bellowed, and that was the last thing I understood before they launched into Greek. Screaming at each other in their language. My mother, sounding more like a native than anyone would believe, faster and faster, and I could visualise the hand gestures.

I sat cross legged on the floor outside the room as they batted back and forth, picking up only a few words, that by the time my brain had translated them, had become stale and out of context. I supposed it didn't really matter what they were saying, as long as they did. I supposed it made no difference if I heard them or not, I was just used to knowing everything. It was almost a relief.

But I felt lonely, sitting outside on my own as my family adopted strangers' voices to argue. I wondered if he did it on purpose, if he knew I was listening and didn't want me to know. I knew that no matter what now, I would never gain that language, never own it the way Nicky had. He was Greek, through and through. He had been taught it by Yiayia, spoken to, sung to, conversed with. He had known it before he knew English. I would never have that, unless I lived there for years. And I couldn't bear the thought of that, especially as it was so easy to speak English there now.

No way to lay claim to that, a language to shout at my mother in, a language no-one could keep secrets from me in. Mine.

That one phrase rolled around and around in my head, somehow painful, a recognisable anguish though the words had yet to come. I sat there for at least half an hour, as their voices rose, and trembled and fell again, soft, cajoling tones, harsh, passionate ones.

Then ego dipota.

I have nothing, my brother had said. I have nothing.

Chapter Forty-Two

I am fourteen when we go to the Northern Side. Dad's outraged, Mum's curious. Nicky stays silent, as usual. It looks the same as the South, obviously, but the light is somehow greyer here, and whilst they retained some of the most beautiful parts of the island, it just feels wrong to me.

Yiayia doesn't come on holiday this year, but she's excited for us. She congratulates my mother on convincing Dad to go across the border, to try new things. She gives us great big lists of the beautiful places she remembers from childhood, wrote precise directions in her language that Mum keeps in her purse. Her cousins' houses, her auntie's family. Take pictures of their houses to show her, bring them back and let them compare. She tells us this with absolutely no anger, no resentment. She's used to it.

Because her aunties and cousins could never return to their homes, to that side of the island. Did we really want to see a family home inhabited by strangers? Taken by force?

In a lot of cases, a nice Turkish family would let in these nervous Greek strangers, almost apologetic for how their ancestors gained that land, for how they inherited their home.

Others would simply ignore the little old ladies dressed in black, staring up at them from the front garden, remembering their lives in that house. Raising their children, Easter feasts and barbecues every weekend in July.

Yiayia was eager to know what everything looked like, and we knew straight away we wouldn't tell her about the military presence, the bomb sites they had surrounded with casinos, the machine guns as you crossed the check-point.

The family homes sold illegally to English tourists, who had no idea they were buying stolen land. Buying memories and converting them to holiday homes. A war? An invasion? I don't know what they think, that we shared the island, that it had always been that way? That no-one was at fault. It seems strange to me that perhaps there are people out there who think Cyprus is a Turkish island, that they never even thought of the South.

And worst of all, a picture that won't leave my mind, when you cross the border that garish flag carved into the mountainside. Could there be a clearer sign of their destruction, their true intentions? They saw it as dominance, no doubt-claim the mountain, claim the land. But really, cutting away into nature, something awe-inspiring that's been there for longer that we existed? Paint the rocks a toxic red and white, suffocate them amongst a naturally green landscape. Not a Turkish flag, a Turkish Cypriot flag. Their symbol on our white background. A poke in the face, a two finger's up at the Greeks from the five-fingered mountain.

I wonder how much it cost them. It says 'we are proud of what we did'.

All I feel the whole time is this uncomfortable tugging in my chest and stomach, constricted and sick. A sense of loss, and I don't even know of what. Like an old relative that I'd heard so many wonderful stories about, but would never get to meet, had just died.

We returned to the South that evening in a dull haze, surrounded by English tourists who commented on the beauty of the landscape, how cheap the property was. A holiday home, perhaps, they'd seen them advertised.

Every mountaintop saw new developments crop up, little white blocks in the dark soil.

They bought shisha pipes, bought as many packets of cigarettes as they could get through the checkpoint. Souvenirs that proclaimed 'I went to Cyprus' and all I wanted to scream was 'this isn't Cyprus! It's a lie, a poor impersonation. It's Turkey with a friendly face.'

We stepped off the bus, emotionally exhausted. Drained.

'The things that drives me crazy,' Nicky says quietly, 'is that Turkish people used to live on the South Side, and had to go North after the war. It was a swap. But the Greek government is protecting the Turkish houses in the South. If anyone lives in one of those houses, they're not allowed to change it in any way.'

'It's called being the bigger person,' my father sighs, 'and sometimes, it's a fucking joke.'

My mother shrugs, guilty for starting this whole thing. If we hadn't seen, we would never have felt like this. Angry, on the verge of tears. Agitated and helpless.

We don't feel hungry after that, but we go to the *taverna* anyway. Piled high plates of succulent meat in rich red sauces, bottles of wine from the local vineyard. Shot glasses of *retsina*, given on the house, that Nicky lights on fire before downing. He always looks so typically Greek, so obviously fitting. Like he awakens and becomes who he really is over here, just like Yiayia always has. Waking in the sunshine, with his tanned skin and dark eyes, talking with emotive hand gestures. Speaking louder, laughing often.

We pick at dips with toasted pitta, down glass after glass of water to help with the intense heat. Even in the evening, there is no breeze. We watch as the dancers, dressed in traditional clothing, bright reds and darkest blues do the moves I've seen my entire life. Faster and faster, over chairs, balancing glasses. It never fails to enchant me. They move to music that doesn't seem to court them, just gets faster, more desperate, until they're swirling in the middle of a circle, sweat pouring off of them. A man from the band walks up to the head dancer, and sticks a note to his forehead. Five Cypriot pounds. It stays. His sweat has proven his hard work, has earned his tip. The whole crowd claps along from their tables, English, Greek, whoever. Some get up and have a go. The Greeks call *bravo, opa!* the whooping of unintelligible excitement. We do not talk about the Northern Side. We do not mention politics, or the possibility of Turkish entry to the EU, or anything important. Politics is saved for late in the evening, for old men talking over games of *tavli* and Metaxa brandy, until they shrug their shoulders and give up, sure there will never be an answer.

For now, it was time to dance.

Chapter Forty-Three

Drugs are easy enough to find if you know how to talk to people. Well, drug people. It's like a secret language, a subculture, a society. We are We, and You are You. Sometimes, they cross over, but not always. Go to Camden, see a dodgy guy about a hallucinatory dog. Or something.

When you're a girl it's different though, more dangerous. You have to choose someone pathetic, a dealer you know can't hurt you. Although this usually means you're sacrificing quality for safety. But what can you do?

The forty days were almost done, so close to colour returning, to everything moving fast again. But I hadn't learnt anything, hadn't made sense of it yet. She was gone, and what? Dad was out and Mum was there, and Nicky was locked away, and there was Daniel, hanging around like he might be permanent. Life goes on, as they say.

So I had an idea. A stupid fuckwit idea. Something that was likely to be a big mistake. But it seemed right to me. It made sense. So I scored from this pikey fucker under the bridge, and sat in a cafe, and decided to see how it felt. Valium. Well, whatever street level version was going. If I could take it and then turn away, then I wasn't her. I wasn't numb, I wasn't unhappy. It would be proof. And by taking it, I was one step closer to her. I would understand her, understand that wash of happiness she'd lived in for over thirty years. How it felt to be her, to be just okay all the time.

So, deep breath and down it goes. Washed down with a cup of coffee, in a greasy spoon, surrounded by builders on their breaks, drinking tea and eating bacon. Except it was all wrong, because I should take it with a glass of *commanderia*, and I should be wearing a red dress. Should be in a home, warm, full of people who loved me but I couldn't connect to. I should be her, I was her. And as I waited to come up, I realised, I didn't want to do a Dex. Didn't want to let something that could be great be lonely. Except wasn't that the point, for it to be bad? So I knew was stronger. But also...I had someone to call. And that wasn't new, because I'd always had people. But I didn't feel like I was a burden, or if I was, it was okay. Because he didn't think that.

So I got on a bus to South London, to Daniel.

And when I got there, wobbling in front of him, bracing myself on his door frame, he raised his eyebrows, smiled, and made me tea. And we waited, together. No television, no blaring music. We cooked dinner, spicy food that filled the little flat with exotic smells, that took time and effort and was actually enjoyable. And if I did come up, I didn't really feel it. We ate and laughed and talked, and his eyes were on me, waiting for that moment, and when it didn't seem to happen, he still kept watching. Eventually we just sat together on the sofa, and I curled so tightly around him that I thought I'd never want to be alone again, never a single entity, surviving on my own. People were made to live in packs, be part of a family, be a group. I started shivering slightly, and he held me closer until I fell asleep, restless but exhausted.

'My brother said Valium is the closest thing to heroin. The feeling, I mean.' It was the morning, and I was colder than I'd ever been, even whilst stealing most of Daniel's body heat.

'Interesting family,' he played with a strand of my hair and knew not to look at me.

'You have no idea.'

214

'Oh, I think I do,' he half-laughed, and I realised I wanted to know about him, his weird family, but he cut me off with the next question, the point.

'Did you learn anything, with this big gesture? Find out what you needed?'

I twitched my mouth in consideration.

'No, nothing. I'm not even sure anything happened.'

'It did. I watched the change. Plus, you took the amount she would have taken, right, your grandmother? Valium doesn't give you a high, it edges off the lows, and the highs, so you're constantly in the middle. Everything's fine, pleasant. Nothing's so painful you can't take it, and nothing's too wonderful to bear. Everything's just okay.'

He pulled me up from the tiny sofa, and towards the bed, where we dove under the covers. He closed his eyes immediately, heavy arm slung over me. Everything's just okay. Just okay, nothing more. Somehow, that was worse. The words rolled around, echoed and bounced around my brain as I looked through that memory bank for Yiayia, for a smile that was real, for excitement or pure joy. Instead I found quiet affection and satisfaction. I didn't want that. I wasn't her, I wouldn't ever be her. I wanted more than okay.

I turned over to face Daniel, and trailed my fingertips across his skin, always drawn to that hidden angry writing on his arm. *The world has let me down.* And yet he was the happiest person I knew. For absolutely no reason. He was light and true smiles, and telling the truth. And he got angry and bugged me until I told him stuff. But when I did, he never judged me. He was happy. And I suddenly realised how easy it was.

I held tight to his arm and just looked at him, trying to make him understand.

He stared back, blue-eyed boy, scanning my face for a signal, a sign that something was wrong, or right, or anything. I smiled and kissed him. I placed his arms around me, his hands on the small of my back, where I felt safest, protected. Cold hands, warm body.

And I didn't think of letting go of Dex, or what my Dad would have said, or what my grandmother had done. I just felt this bursting rush of something, something that was maybe love.

It wasn't perfect, and it wasn't about feeling wanted or feeling pretty, but about the way his rough fingertips traced my skin, how he looked at me the whole time, like he really saw me.

The weight of him, warm and heavy and so much stronger than me. Burning kisses that seared my skin, scarring until I was desperate for him. Desperate for fingertips that dug into me, held me so close I could feel every tense of his muscles until I gasped for breath. Skin on skin delicious and the sounds I made that didn't sound like me.

But it was when he smiled into my mouth and scrunched up his face, fiddling one-handed with the foil wrapper that I thought he might be perfect. I muffled my laughter in his neck, tracing a vein with my tongue, biting gently.

His eyes were close to mine, until the blue was a blur and his eyelashes touched mine.

'You're sure?' he breathed.

'Now is not the time for stupid questions,' I pulled him closer, shaking with anticipation. I wasn't comparing it to last time, it wasn't even the same game as before. I felt everything.

I sighed into his mouth as his thumb slipped under my waistband, and he pulled back to look at me when I gasped. Concern and surprise relaxed into a lazy smile, pleased with himself. Pleased with me. I kissed him so he couldn't keep looking at me like that.

I didn't feel empty, or numb or okay at all. I felt alight, alive. I would get hurt, of course, one day things would fall apart. But for now, it was real.

The little white room with the green curtains that kept the light out, the place I could hide, where I finally exorcised that ghost. Not hers, but someone I thought I loved once. I thought briefly of Dex afterwards, and then didn't think of him again. I traced those words of the man who had been hurt, and felt suddenly so painfully naively sure that he could look after me. That he wanted to, and that I would let him.

When he told me he loved me, he wasn't high on anything. When I replied, I wasn't lying.

Chapter Forty-Four

It's been exactly a year since Pappou died, although I'm too young to know this at the time. Nothing much has changed, except the arm chair in the corner of the room is empty most of the time. My father has taken to saying 'I don't like you, but I love you', as a joke, or to keep the memory alive. Most of the time I don't like it. Some days I see the funny side. It's got to be hard to love someone you don't like.

Me and Gali talk about it sometimes. We really want to say we loved him, it seems like the right response when people ask us if we miss him. But we never really knew him. The salacious stories won't surface for years, and by the time they do, we're too old to be really interested. Gali will have boys chasing her, falling for those bright eyes and cheeky smile. She's never shy with them. I'll have found disposable friends and casual drug use, the excitement of the eighth double-vodka-redbull and the moment you can't stop shaking, so you just have to dance. We'll both become masters in hiding who we really are from our family. Her, because they think she's shy, and me, because no-one could imagine me any other way.

But for now, the Big House is calm, and Nicky's back, being fattened up. Sticky Greek cakes, and third helpings of soup. Kebabs in toasted pittas and potatoes cooked in a clay pot. Mum says nothing about the fact that since Nicky's been back he stays at Yiayia's almost all the time. Eats the food she prepares for him, instead of eating at home with us, sleeps there instead of the old box room with the Smiths posters, the bed still made with the bright blue sheets he had as a kid.

Nicky smiles at Yiayia, like the prized child he is. The boy, the eldest. First grandchild, favoured one. But we can't be jealous, me and Gali, we love him too. How could we not? Nicky, who always came searching for us during hide and seek, and would never leave us sitting silently for an hour in the laundry cupboard whilst he went to talk to the adults. He never treated us like stupid kids.

Yiayia's face is always kindest when it's focused on Nicky. We know she loves us too, but that smile is purely for him, like he saved her once, like she can't thank him enough for something. *Lavendi-mou, lavendi,* the favoured chant, the prayer. The words are plain enough, and yet could mean anything. My boy, my lovely boy, my little soldier, my grown man.

She walks around the house as if surveying for dirt, and as Gali and Nicky race to eat their soup, I follow her from the kitchen. She straightens curtains, and plumps pillows. Runs one finger across the edges for dust.

And then I watch as she gets to the picture of Pappou on the mantle. She traces the picture with her fingertips, but there's no smile on her face. Instead, her features harden, and she suddenly sticks her tongue out at the photograph. She sees me looking and winks, before placing the photograph face-down in the drawer.

She walks back to the kitchen, slowly, and pours us each a glass of commanderia, mine and Gali's literally measured out with a thimble she kept in the cutlery drawer for just such occasions. Nicky gets more, obviously.

She raises her glass, and we copy her.

'*Stelli-yassas!*' she says, and we repeat, and clink.

'To freedom!' she says to herself, smiling, as she serves up homemade cake, and we let it soak up the wine in our mouths that we couldn't bear to swallow.

Chapter Forty-Five

I'd woken up with Daniel, allowing that pervading sense that everything was perfect to engulf me. Normally I'd have run away from it, convinced myself it wasn't as good as it seemed, and that everything would have a comedown. But I couldn't help it.

I lay in that warm bed that smelled like him, and he didn't ruin it. He didn't start playing guitar or discuss those poetry books on the shelf above his bed. He didn't joke about last night. All he did was roll over, kiss my neck and sigh. Then he slapped me on the arse and went to make tea. And I knew it would be alright.

And somehow, stepping outside and leaving that room wasn't a big deal. I left mid-morning after lazy kisses and words whispered with my eyes closed. I left my bag there, nowhere near the door.

I got the tube, then the bus, and got off two stops early and walked the rest. Opened the front door, and walked slowly up to my room, nodding at my reflection in the mirror in the hall. My hair was longer, the tips curling up. Just different enough, still me.

I started to paint, the canvas blankly beautiful, awaiting my ideas. And I knew exactly what to do, what to make, and why. I opened my windows wide, and even though it wasn't sunny out, it was bright and light and warm. There was no music, no drugs, nothing but exactly what I was feeling and exactly what the brush was doing.

Dad barged in after about twenty minutes, irritated and unsure, shifting his weight from foot to foot, screwing up his eyes at the smell of acrylics.

'You didn't come home last night.'

I didn't even look, 'I don't come home a lot of nights, Dad.'

'But now you have a boyfriend.'

'Do you want me to say I stayed at Lee's? I can, if that makes you happier.'

'I want you to start respecting me.' He tried to sound stern, but I heard the wobble in his voice.

I didn't dare to look away from the paint as I replied.

'Then start being someone I can respect.'

Sad, weak little man with your greying hair and scrabble for control. Small man, weak lies. Silly billy. I didn't look up as the door slammed, but I could breathe again. My room, my painting, my life. No outsiders welcome, family or not. Just the weave of the canvas, the smell of the paint. The light blues, the whites of the eyes. Red edges, blurring in with the thousands of shades of blues, swirling in together, becoming everything I was ever sure of. Blue, true, inescapable. The sea, the sky, the perfect eyes of a strange boy. That point when your heart drops into your stomach, and your veins throb with how much you don't care. The colour of the carpet in the Big Old House, the evil eyes chinking in the light of the kitchen, the first dress I wore and loved, exactly the same as Gali's. That cloud that I lived in until the morning Yiayia died.

Mum was the next in, knocking gently, but walking in without waiting for a response. She was about to start talking, but instead saw the painting, the outline of the face in greys and olives against the blues, and sighed.

'It's depressing,' she shook her head.

'It's true,' I replied, 'besides, it's not finished. You might like it once it's done.'

She shrugged, 'Well either way, it's nice to see you doing something creative.'

I smiled at her, my beautiful mother who looked so worn down with the energy it took to be positive. Trying to be supportive, trying to believe the best of everyone. She rubbed at the little daisy outline under her hair, and smiled back, like she was completely making it up as she went along. Which she probably was.

'You're very talented, darling, I hope we've told you that enough,' she paused, her hand on the door, 'I'm glad you're not going to law school. It's not really you, is it?'

I shook my head, suddenly so desperate for those days when I could curl up with my mother in front of the television and fall asleep in her lap. For those times when I was so at ease, so comfortable to be looked after, and didn't have to think about anyone else's happiness. To be a small child in grown-up arms. To breathe deeply, smell the same perfume and know that everything would be alright because my mama said so.

She stroked my hair and walked out, leaving the door open. I shut it gently behind her.

Hours had passed by the time Nicky looked in, and the painting was almost finished. I was sitting on my bed staring at it when his knock came, hesitant and gentle. He waited until I had called for him to come in, and then he sat down next to me, silent, analysing it the same way I was. But I knew as I was questioning the colours, the lines, the shading, he saw only what I meant it to be.

'It's beautiful,' he said quietly.

'Mum thinks it's depressing,' I half-smiled and nudged him.

'Nah, it's just...her. It's completely her.'

He put his arm around me, and I felt like that kid again, desperate for his attention, his approval.

'So, you're an artist, little sister.'

'I guess I am, but what am I going to do as a career?' I put my head on his shoulder.

'Whatever makes you money and makes you happy, I guess.'

'And you?'

'Actually, I've had a breakthrough in that, I think.'

He turned to face me, and I felt one word rise up from the back of my brain, wrapped in panic. *Manchester.* He was leaving again.

'I'm going to Cyprus.'

I blinked at him, tilted my head to the side. Well, a holiday, away from the parents, connect with the family, see the old village where our grandparents grew up. That made sense.

'I'm going to join the army.'

My stomach dropped. 'What?'

'I'm not too old yet for National Service over there. They tried to recruit me before, but I had a pass as a British citizen. They'll still take me, if I ask.'

'You want to join the army? The army? I thought you were a pacifist?' I heard my voice shaking, shrill, completely irrational.

'I am. They'll never go to war, Ellie. Never. It's too politically tied up. But there's training. There's discipline, no chance to go off the rails. No time in between running for miles and shining your boots to miss getting high. I need it. I need someone to tell me what to do, every hour of every day. I need it.'

I felt sick, worried, lost. But it made sense. My brother knew how to protect himself, how to protect everyone from him. He always came back. He always came back. He wouldn't leave me, he promised.

'Don't worry about me.' He put his arm around me again, 'it's all going to be fine, really. Everything will be just fine.'

'Just fine. Nothing better?' My throat choked.

'Let's aim for survival. Everything else is a bonus.' He kissed me on both cheeks, old-fashioned Greek boy, and I wondered if he'd come back one of those masochists, the puffed up fast-talking boys who suddenly expect a wife or mother to do everything for them. Who believe they've done something important, playing with guns on an imaginary battlefield. If he'd ever be our Nicky again.

'Wish me luck, I'm off to tell Mum.' He squeezed my hand and slipped out of the room. He could never be anything but our Nicky. And if I closed my eyes he was right there, in the sunshine, by the sand and the sea. Home. Mum was going to freak out.

I looked back at the painting, Yiayia's knowing eyes watching everything that had just happened, smiling beyond the blues that swirled around her, dark and dangerous and enveloping. Beautiful, but sad. *Melancholia*, she called it. Balance of sadness and exaltation, ecstasy and desperation. Her dark days, her blue days, her melancholy. Her face didn't smile from the painting, it looked proud, kind, important. Nothing like me. I missed her, I missed all the things I'd never know about her. But at least I felt it.

Chapter Forty-Six

He's wearing a black t-shirt, and his teeth are really straight. I can't tell what colour his eyes are in the club, but they're light. I find myself hoping they're blue. He's the one, my Friday Night Friend.

I smile and nod along with the music, that coming up like a deep breath and an expansion of your heart that I imagine love feels like. He doesn't do anything but watch for a while, but I keep an eye on him. That one. He's the one to talk to, he's coming up too. He'll keep my secrets. He'll know all of me. And then he'll be gone.

We talk outside, whilst Lee smokes a cigarette and he comes to bum a light. Except he spends more time talking than actually smoking it. I briefly hope it's a line. We talk about how beautiful the stars look from the cramped smoking area, where we can just about look up. We talk about whether there's parallel versions of us standing in this very spot in an alternate reality, or whether we'd have met somewhere else. We talk about science fiction, and TV and whether music would exist if there were no drugs.

His friends snicker, and I wonder if they've spiked him, that he's not a regular at this. But he takes my hand, and squeezes in time to the beat. He bangs one hand against his knee as a drum rhythm. It's out of time, and I find my face aching from how much I'm smiling.

We share a bottle of water, and he tells me his name is Daniel. I won't remember it.

We decide to get out of there, go back to his, and we chat like maniacs on the bus route home, and not once does the paranoia return, not once do I feel scared that I'm leaving with a complete stranger. Which is ridiculous, because I spend all my time feeling scared. That doing anything is doing something dangerous. That I'm foolish and young and lost.

He makes cups of tea, and we drink half a cup each before realising he forgot to boil the kettle. I don't say anything. He tells me he believes in destiny. I tell him I might hate my father. He tells me his mother abandoned him. I tell him I don't belong to my own culture. He tells me he loves me. I tell him the same.

The usual Friday night, when I know I will wake up tomorrow, and go back to my life. Closed off and cold, with unhappy parents, and a best friend who's never loved me back.

Except, as I chew another piece of gum and nod my head as he plays the guitar badly, I have trouble even visualising tomorrow. My heart races, and the clock says four am.

It's the first time I've ever wanted to kiss one of my strangers.

Chapter Forty Seven

It was the day of the *mimosino*, the day we said goodbye. The sun was shining too brightly, and it was the last day we would wear black. Everyone was dark, dark haired, dark skinned, dark suits with oversized sunglasses. I clicked into my familiar, painful heels and stood in the hallway, waiting for my family. Nicky thumped downstairs, straight-backed, eyes forward, straightening his tie. My fingers fidgeted to fix it, but it was perfect the way it was. Mum primped in the smudged glass of the kitchen cabinets, pulling her hair down over her tattoo, rubbing that tiny outline of black on pure white skin. I tousled my own hair as I watched her, aware of it growing out, not so harsh now, rather soft and curling under my earlobes. Dad had spent an hour shining his shoes, and checking his phone every five minutes. He walked out of the room to take a call, and I watched him. When he returned, I didn't look away, and he nodded, turning his phone off and holding it up for me to see.

We drove to the church in silence, Dad unsure of what to say, Mum not talking to Nicky, Nicky seeing no need to break the quiet. I sat and thought of meeting my friends in the pub that night, the fact that Dex had asked Mona, and she'd wanted to come. That she'd made a little book of my sketches at *Baby's,* added dialogue and subtitles. She wanted to send it off, get it printed. She thought people needed to see it. She was bringing it to the pub. I was going to say yes. I was always going to say yes, as often as I possibly could. Mags and Lee would be showing pictures of the flat they wanted, down from the bridge in the market. I'd told Daniel they'd be better off on a barge, never settling, never getting stuck anywhere.

And Daniel, well, he'd be there. At the pub, at his flat, anywhere I wanted him to be. And he'd always be remembered, as my artist, my collaborator. Because hidden on the inside of my ankle was one word, in the most beautiful writing he could create, like ink had fallen into words on my skin, desperate for definition. *Persephone.* For her, for me. For the changing seasons and the love in the darkness.

The church was busy, all the cousins and aunties and uncles with the same names, kissing on both cheeks, talking about their families, about Yiayia, about the everyday, stupid things. And I couldn't hate them for it, because I did it too. It's what you did. Better than standing there, saying inanely sentimental things about who she was, and what she stood for, because who really knows that? Who truly knows anything about anybody? All we knew is we loved her, completely, and for once, that was enough.

The family filled the pews, but it was Sunday service, and the place was packed. Me and Nicky leant against the back wall, cold and solid and there for centuries. Lost in the half-song, half-cries of the Orthodox church. That language that was his, was suddenly mine, because he didn't understand it either. He knew when to make the sign of the cross, when to bow his head. And I watched him, as I had when I was a child, following his orders, Simon Says. He opened his eyes, head still bowed, and winked at me. I reached over and squeezed his hand.

My legs ached, and my heels squeaked and I couldn't even notice the distinctions in the church service and the listing of the names, and when it finally came, I expected to feel nothing. Everything was fine, more or less. The names of the dead, the names of the lost, the names of those who've left us behind, left us missing them. The same few names over and over again, because everyone is named after someone else. So typically Greek. *Eleni Kazakis.* We heard it. I looked to Nicky, who shrugged. We watched as our father's rigid back suddenly slumped, like something had released. For everyone else, it was like nothing had happened, and really, nothing had. I heard my name sung out in a way it never was before, in mourning, in ceremony. I heard my name, and something ended. Like a drop in my stomach, an acid fizzle, a sudden realisation. She was gone, and it didn't really matter why.

We hung around at the back as a wave of little old ladies rushed forward for communion. Big men in black holding their children up high, passing them towards the alter. The glory of God, the blessings of their culture. We clung together, Gali and Nicky and me, watching as everyone else moved around us, and I fingered the warm cold cross around my neck. She'd given it to me, she'd given them to all of us, Christening gifts. Gali and me held hands until we left the church.

As I hobbled down the steps from the church in my heels, the wind ruffled my heavy winter coat, revealing the red dress underneath. My mother should have tutted, my father shake his head with the impropriety of it, the disrespect of defying tradition. But they said nothing. My father just stroked my cheek, and told me I looked so much like her. I knew then that things would never be just fine. We would have wrenching pain and anger and love and beauty and death, and everything as it should be. Yiayia's voice echoed in my mind with those nonsense words, that language that was no-one's. *Kounia bella, omorfi gobella*...always swinging back and forth, safe, always safe, but always afraid of falling.

There was one time I knew she was happy. Not just content, or okay, not another day of 'I alright, dahlink, I alright' but truly, madly happy. When she was by the sea. Not cooking, or singing, or teaching us things, but one stark moment in my memory when she stood on the beach when the tide came in, pulled down her hat, and smiled at the sun. A late afternoon in Cyprus, when she took off her sunglasses and looked back at us, beckoned us into the water with her. Her light eyes looking at us with wonder, gesturing as if she couldn't quite believe what surrounded her. And we laughed, squealed, splashed through the water until it came up to our waists, reaching for her. She laughed. When the sea wasn't dark and dangerous, or aquamarine calm, but clear, pure, empty. Blue.

Other publications available from Stairwell Books

First Tuesday in Wilton	Ed. Rose Drew and Alan Gillott
The Exhibitionists	Ed. Rose Drew and Alan Gillott
The Green Man Awakes	Ed. Rose Drew
Carol's Christmas	N.E. David
Fosdyke and Me and Other Poems	John Gilham
frisson	Ed. Alan Gillott
Feria	N.E. David
Along the Iron Veins	Ed. Alan Gillott and Rose Drew
A Day at the Races	N.E. David
Gringo on the Chickenbus	Tim Ellis
Running With Butterflies	John Walford
Foul Play	P. J. Quinn
Late Flowering	Michael Hildred
Scenes from the Seedy Underbelly of Suburbia	Jackie Simmons
Pressed by Unseen Feet	Ed. Rose Drew and Alan Gillott
York in Poetry Artwork and Photographs	Ed. John Coopey and Sally Guthrie
Poison Pen	P.J.Quinn
Rosie and John's Magical Adventure	The Children of Ryedale District Primary Schools

For further information please contact rose@stairwellbooks.com

www.stairwellbooks.co.uk